Going Ghost

A Paranormal Cozy Mystery

Dina Marie

ISBN: 978-1-964858-00-5 (ebook)

ISBN: 978-1-964858-01-2 (paperback)

Book cover design by Elizabeth Mackey

For Mom

Chapter 1

I RAN UP THE cracked concrete steps of the old, historic home with my head down, rain dripping off my blond wig. This wasn't the way I envisioned visiting Salem, Massachusetts. I had imagined selfie-filled tours dressed as Winifred Sanderson of *Hocus Pocus*. Gorging on New England clam chowder until I was fat and happy. Traipsing around downtown with an ice cream cone in hand and without a care in the world.

Instead, here I was. Out of breath. Nearly out of money. Soaking wet. And totally starving.

Not to mention a husband who would, in all likelihood, kill me if he found me. When I say *kill*, I mean that literally. He threatened it repeatedly. And I believed him. Not that anyone would believe *me*. My husband was quite charismatic—incredibly good-looking, a favorite at parties. The kind of guy who would shovel snow from your sidewalk before even thinking about clearing his own. A regular beau of the ball. Meanwhile, he harbored a dirty little secret: *he likes to control his wife. And smack her around from time to time.* Little did I know when I married Joe eight years ago that he would take the words "till death do us part" as some kind of challenge. Boy, I really knew how to pick 'em.

But enough about him. I had a new life to embark on.

I tried jamming my key into the lock, but it didn't seem to fit. Had I copied the wrong one? No way. I had memorized the key's every nook and cranny in the six months I had been planning this little escape. I glanced at the address on the placard affixed to the building's brick facade. This was the place. *I could feel it.*

I looked around me. Luckily, the entrance to the house was not street-facing but in a side driveway that was wide enough for an economy car but narrow enough to shield me from pedestrians. Not surprisingly, though, not many folks wanted to take Salem tours at ten o'clock at night in the pouring rain.

I glanced at the building next door, half-expecting to see Joe staring at me, but the inside lights were off, and there was no Ring doorbell to document my every move. Good. I hated those things.

I inhaled deeply, held the key with both hands, and managed to get it into the lock. *Yay.* I pressed to the left and was surprised when the key turned left with me. *Double yay.* I pushed into the wooden door that was badly in need of a coat of paint, but nothing happened.

Was it stuck? I gave it another shove, and a pain shot through my shoulder, but the door was still closed tight.

I should have gone to the gym more often.

I planted my feet firmly on the top step, adjusted the straps of my backpack, and threw my petite, size-8 body against the chipped wood with all my might. It swung open into the darkness, and I fell with it onto a cold, dusty—and extremely hard—wood floor. But there was no time for assessing my injuries.

Quickly, I got up, closed the door, slid the deadbolt back into place, and crouched down under the door's smudged window, looking outside. Satisfied that the driveway was still empty, I dropped my backpack to the floor and breathed a sigh of relief.

Welcome home.

For now.

The only problem was, I had no idea what this home was. Not only had I never been here before—I hadn't been *anywhere* in the last eight years—I couldn't see a thing. The light coming from the streetlights, trickling in between the closed shades and the window frames, revealed nothing but shadows. Big, creepy shadows.

Relax. There's nothing to be afraid of. For once.

Easier said than done. My heart was beating violently, as if I had just run a marathon. In some ways, I had. Today's journey had taken me across three states, often by foot, and involved three different clothing changes. I peered out the smudged window again. The driveway was still empty. No sound of footsteps. I pulled my knees into my chest and then pulled off the blond wig, which had been making my head itch all day. I tossed it into the darkened room and yanked out every bobby pin I could find, letting my red tresses escape their oppression. I leaned my head against the door.

You're okay.

I closed my eyes to keep my imagination from turning those shadows across the room into monsters and listened to the rain pound against the building.

I used to love the rain.

I used to love my husband.

I used to love my life.

I used to love a great many things before my sentencing (wedding day) eight years ago, but I was too tired to remember any of them. Running away from home wasn't as exciting as the movies made it out to be. It was exhausting and stressful.

But for the first time in eight years, three days, and—I looked at my watch—eight hours, I could close my eyes without worrying whether I had mistakenly left the cap off the toothpaste or left the light on in the basement. I didn't have to worry about the needle on the gas tank of the BMW dipping under a quarter tank or smudges on the refrigerator door handle. Yes, I was sitting in an old, dark, historic home that was probably haunted, and I had little money and little idea of where I was going next, but that beat having to sleep next to a monster who had no qualms about taking his anger or insecurities or whatever his problem was out on the person he was supposed to love most in the world.

And with that happy thought, I pulled my backpack toward me, lay down on the cold, hard floor that had probably already ruined my back, wrapped my arms around myself to stem the shivering, and fell fast asleep.

Chapter 2

A voice startled me.

I opened my eyes and immediately tried to stand, but something was on me, constricting me like bubble wrap. I instinctively thrust out my arms and legs like an MMA fighter until whatever it was came off me. Then I stood up and, dare I say, put my hands in the air in a victory stance. Over the past eight years, I had learned to celebrate any victory, big or small. Sneaking a visit to my father while Joe was at the dentist. Scarfing down a hot dog while Joe made a trip to the bathroom at a party.

I looked down at the antagonist I had conquered: a thick, woolly, and moldy-smelling blanket, which was lying crumpled at my feet.

Where the heck did that come from?

To my right was a stack of blankets about four feet high, next to an empty garbage pail. Maybe one had fallen on me, and in my sleep I had the good sense to spread it over me. Probably saved me from getting pneumonia.

"Have a good day, Charlie!"

The voice. There it was again.

I crouched against the door and peered out the grimy window, rubbing the compass pendant around my neck between my index finger and thumb. An old man was letting himself into the house next door. I could see him only from the back, where his hunched shoulders were dotted with raindrops. He hobbled inside, and as he turned to close the door, I lowered myself so he wouldn't see me. Once the coast was clear, I turned around and inspected my temporary living quarters.

Dust.

As far as the eye could see.

On the floor. On the furniture. On the railing of the stairway. I reached out and ran my finger along the top of the small dining table that was nearby, and a coating of the stuff covered my finger.

I imagined Joe's reaction to all this grime. He probably would have a coronary, the neat freak. I was inclined to leave it all where it was or, even better, lather it over my body in some kind of childish act of defiance. As pleasant as that thought was, though, it probably wasn't too healthy having all this dust around, especially if I was planning to live here for a few days. I would have to try to clean up a bit.

At the other end of the room was a wall with five large windows facing the street. Luckily, dusty shades covered them so no one could see in, but that could be a problem at night. I would have to keep the lights off. I flicked a light switch next to the front door and looked up at the ceiling fixture, if you could call it that since it was just a pair of bare bulbs. Nothing. I flicked again and again as if that would solve the problem.

Well, worrying about outsiders seeing interior lighting at night wasn't going to be a problem. Unsurprisingly, there was no electricity.

Right now, though, the morning sun was shining brightly on the front of the house and lighting up the room just a little with whatever rays managed to sneak in. In entirely different circumstances, I could imagine myself getting rid of those dreary shades and buying some pretty valances and blinds that I could open and close when the mood struck.

My body relaxed slightly. This little plan of mine might work. I hadn't ventured upstairs yet, but so far, this seemed like a decent place to hide.

Creak . . .

I had spoken too soon.

I looked up at the ceiling. Whatever relaxation my body had adopted made a beeline for the door after hearing that noise. *Was someone upstairs?*

My first thought went to Joe. But that couldn't be. There was no chance he beat me here. I had several hours' jump on him. Someone else? The house hadn't been lived in for years—at least twenty. I was sure of it. I would have overheard Joe mention something to his realtor. And it certainly didn't *look* like anyone lived here, unless you counted an extended family of dust bunnies. It must have just been the house settling, as they said. These old homes were full of all kinds of creaks and groans.

Or maybe it was a mouse. I looked at the floor. Had one crawled on me while I was sleeping? Gross—and yet still preferable to sleeping next to Joe.

I caught myself. *Be reasonable. Do you see any tiny footprints? Any droppings?* No. And there didn't seem to be the usual things that attracted mice like garbage, food, clutter, or warmth. Why would they bother with this place? No one else seemed to. There was no mouse until I saw a mouse. I refused to live my life in fear anymore. If I did, what had been the purpose of running? I was done running.

If the lights weren't working, I'd have to find a way to get light inside the house. I could open the shades a little during the day. Without any interior lighting, there was little chance anyone would notice me in here, but little chance was too much chance. Plus, I didn't want to change the building facade at all. No need for unwanted attention or prying eyes.

I opened a few kitchen cabinets and found some old dishes and cups but nothing else of interest. An old candle rested on the top shelf of an antique cabinet, across from the front door, accompanied by a little bench topped with a cushion. At least, I *thought* it was a cushion; it might very well have been several years' worth of dust. The candle looked like it had never been used. I hoped it wasn't decorative. A pretend candle would do me no good in my new pretend life.

I reached up and grabbed it by the circular handle, nearly dropping the darn thing on myself because it was so heavy. No wonder it was on a shelf. Who would want to carry this thing around all the time? On the plus side, who needed a gym when this thing could substitute as a dumbbell? I examined the piece. The good news was the candle was real, and the wick looked eager for some excitement.

I pulled open one of the cabinet's drawers and found several old matchboxes. Did matches have an expiration date? I didn't know, but I was about to find out. I opened one up, pulled out a match, and struck it against the gritty line across the box. It burst into a flame instantly, and I quickly lit the candle before the match changed its mind. The blue flame elongated and turned bright yellow.

I had the urge to do a happy dance. Like Tom Hanks in *Castaway. Fire, I've got fire!*

As I began walking around the room, I felt like Wee Willie Winkie (or was it Jack Be Nimble?) from some old nursery rhyme. All I needed was a nightgown and a nightcap with a pom-pom on the bottom.

Creak . . .

There it was again. I walked toward the narrow stairway that led to the upper floor. The stairs were barely three feet across. Whoever had built this thing long ago hadn't known about the future of the American waistline.

As I began to walk up the steps, the light of the candle flickered. A cold breeze was coming from upstairs. I hoped there wasn't some kind of opening or leak. I imagined flooding from the night before. And that would bring mice. And mold.

I grabbed the dusty blanket I had kicked to the floor and wrapped it around myself, trying not to sneeze, and slowly walked up the stairs. Each footfall sounded like a rusty gate swinging shut. If there had ever been any teenagers living here, they would have had a tough time sneaking out of the house.

I made it to the top of the stairs without seeing any gaping foundational cracks or fissures. So far, so good. To the right of the staircase was a small room. A bathroom. I don't know why I flicked the light switch. I didn't expect it to work, and it didn't. I tried to turn on the cold-water faucet of the pedestal sink, but it was stuck. I put the candle down and used both hands, and the handle turned with a jerk and rusty water shot out of the spigot.

Well, brown water is better than no water.

I peered into the small toilet, which had no water in the bowl. Next to it was a footed bathtub with an old bucket inside. I filled the bucket with water from the sink and poured it into the toilet. Then I lifted the lid of the toilet tank and poured lots of water in there. I pushed the handle of the toilet down, expecting nothing to happen, but the pipes coughed and choked, and the water in the bowl swirled round and round.

Cool. At least the plumbing worked. That would save me from having to try to find a Starbucks every time I had to go.

I picked up the candle and was counting my blessings that I no longer had to worry about any sudden bouts of IBS when I walked out of the bathroom and saw a strange man standing next to a frilly twin bed. He was staring right at me.

Chapter 3

I LET OUT A scream and backed against the wall, holding the candle in front of me as if it were a blowtorch or a fire-breathing dragon, but the man was still, looking at me with curiosity. Good thing because that candle I was holding was more likely to hurt me than him.

"Who are you?" I demanded as if I had every right to be there. "If you're a squatter of some kind, you'll need to leave."

He continued standing, motionless, and I got a better look at him. He was pale. Too pale. Like a hologram. Rays of sunlight streaming through rips in the window shades behind him were shining right through him, making a faint shadow on the wood floor. How could that be? Before I could ask myself any more questions, the man spoke, his voice surprisingly robust.

"'Tis you who trespass upon these grounds, I reckon," he said in some sort of old-fashioned English.

Goosebumps shot up my arms. The silver candleholder shook in my hand. This couldn't be real. Somebody was making a joke. Maybe Joe really *was* here. Messing with me. He had somehow tracked me here and had set up an elaborate prank to scare me. I looked around for a movie projector—the kind recording artists used so they could dance or sing on stage with someone who passed away, like Prince or Frank Sinatra.

But I didn't see anything. And I didn't think I was imagining this. I blinked my eyes. He was still there. I blinked them again. Still there.

Blink.

There.

Blink.

There.

Unfortunately, the only other alternative for this little encounter was something that defied the laws of nature. Something I didn't believe in. Never had. Not even when my mom died, and I prayed for it to be true. That this very, very pale man standing before me in this old, empty home, somehow and in some way, was . . . was . . .

"I go by the name of William. William Kensington." He bowed slightly, his eyes looking through me as if *I* was the one who was transparent.

I was too stunned to speak, so I just stood there, my gaping mouth sucking in the dust in the air. But the longer I stood there, with the silence between us, the weirder I felt. Like I was being rude. And I couldn't have that. My parents had raised me to be polite. Even if this thing in front of me was a figment of my imagination.

Plus, he wasn't wrong. I *was* trespassing. Kind of.

"My name is . . . Clara."

I was sure that, to an outsider, it appeared I was talking to an empty room, but it didn't feel empty. I may have been able to see through William, but his presence was as palpable as if he were filled with blood, water, and human tissue.

He nodded, and I realized his eyes were blue. A pale, but warm blue. Not the White Walker kind from *Game of Thrones*. He shuffled his ghost feet, and that's when I noticed the floor. There were faint footprints in the dust. He was *standing*. Had *he* made the creaky noise? If he was really a ghost (the fact that I was considering this showed me just how delusional I was), would he make footprints? Why walk when you could float? Was it easier on the joints?

"'Tis a pleasure to make your acquaintance. But," William cleared his throat, "you must go."

Weirdly, his voice was saying the words, but there was something about those blue eyes that made me think he didn't mean them. I shook my head. After eight years with Joe, a ghost wasn't going to scare me. (Beyond my initial terror, of course.) I had to stand strong, despite this little paranormal monkey wrench. No more backing down from the things I wanted—I had made a promise to myself ever since I made the decision to leave Joe. "I can't."

This seemed to surprise him. "Pray, wherefore not?"

"I have nowhere else to go at the moment," I said, hoping I'd answered his question. I hadn't watched an old film on TCM in a long time, so I couldn't be sure.

"Whence do you hail? Might you re-traverse your path?"

"No." I had done enough traversing in the past couple of days. "I will never go back there."

He stared into my eyes before looking down at his boots. "Well . . . none are aware of my presence here. Such seclusion suits me well."

"None are aware of my presence here, either. Such seclusion suits me well, too."

My reply appeared to amuse him. He smiled, his ashy lips curving upward and revealing a chipped cuspid tooth. "You converse in a peculiar manner. Akin to a looking glass." He pointed to a floor mirror on a stand in the corner of the room, near a doorway that led to another section of the upper floor.

I was conversing in a peculiar manner? Pot, meet kettle.

"Well," I said, "in some ways, that's what I am. A mirror . . . a looking glass. I learned pretty quickly how to reflect a person's mood back at them. To become what they wanted me to be."

"As amusement?"

"No, for survival. Let's just say my husband isn't such a great guy . . ." I paused. This was the first person . . . er, someone . . . I had made that admission to. "Anyway, I've gotten so good at it that," the candle shook in my hand, "I've forgotten who I am."

William smiled.

"Why is that funny?"

"Your reason lacks truth," he said.

Really? Even male *ghosts* thought they were always right? Death didn't soften their conviction? "You wouldn't know. You don't know me."

He shrugged his square shoulders. "If what you say is true, that you have forgotten who you are, you would not find yourself in this vicinity. If you possess the wisdom to depart whence you came, you are assuredly in possession of your scruples."

I blinked. I hadn't thought of that. And certainly not *like* that. But he was right. As beaten and deflated as I had been over these past eight years, I had always had a plan and the desire to break free. I knew I would one day. I just needed to find my opportunity. Joe hadn't broken me. He certainly made his share of dents, but I was strong (thanks, Mom and Dad!) and could quickly bounce back into place. Like a memory-foam mattress.

We stood there looking at each other, so I figured now was as good a time as any to change the subject. "Do you live here?"

William nodded.

"For how long?"

"A goodly span of time."

Not helpful. "What year do you remember?"

"Eighteen sixty-three."

Eighteen sixty-three? The shock of seeing William having worn off, I looked more closely at him. He appeared to be a few years older than I was, in his late thirties, and was wearing a dark gray flannel coat with (not surprisingly) gray trousers, maybe wool, and some sort of leather boots. An image of my middle school social studies teacher came to mind. "Are you a Civil War soldier?"

The question seemed to perplex him. "I fought in the War of the Rebellion."

Same thing. "You were a Union soldier?"

"Yes, ma'am." His face changed, darkening a little, if that were possible. "But I never desire again to hurt another, or to draw my saber or pistol." He looked at me closely. "We prevailed, yes? In the war?"

"Yes," I said. "The north won."

Satisfied, he nodded his head.

I had the urge to keep talking. Like in the dreams I had with my mother, I didn't want this encounter to end. It wasn't every day you got to chat with someone who used the word *prevailed*. "Have you always been alone?"

"Not in this abode. Others have, over time, taken up residence, only to depart hence."

"You mean, other . . . *ghosts* lived here?" I wasn't sure if I should use that term. Was it impolite?

"No, others akin to yourself."

"Alive humans, you mean?"

"Yes."

So, he lived here once with other people. Got it. "Why haven't you left? You know, gone to . . .?" What was I supposed to say? Heaven? The spiritual realm? Where did people go when they passed on? If anywhere. Best to stay away from the topic of religion. And politics, for that matter. I decided on the spot that social media rules needed to apply when conversing with a ghost. "Are you able to leave the house?"

William looked at the windows where the sun was trying to break in. "Out there?"

"Yes."

"I never made the attempt."

"Really? Why?"

William grew silent, so I pivoted to another topic. "How did you get here?"

This question, too, seemed to make him uncomfortable, but before I could toss up another poor conversation starter, he changed the subject. "How much time has elapsed?"

"Since eighteen sixty-three? A long time. More than a hundred and fifty—"

A dog began barking right outside the window, and as much as the noise startled me, William didn't bat an eyelash. Assuming he had eyelashes. The barks grew louder as a young voice—it sounded like a teenage girl—guided the dog away.

"Such occurrences transpire often," William said. "No cause for undue alarm."

Barking dogs. Great. I had been hoping to get some peaceful sleep around here before I had to pick up and move again. I didn't realize Salem was a town for dogs. Witches, yes. And, apparently, ghosts, but dogs? And then it hit me. The dogs must know William's here. They can probably sense him as they walk by. The poor things were trying to tell their owners day after day during their walks, but the owners weren't listening. I felt for the dogs. I knew what it was like to know a secret and not be able to tell a soul.

The candle was getting heavy in my hands. I had forgotten I was still holding it. I blew out the flame and set it down on a chest of drawers, tightening the blanket around me as William eyed its frayed edges. "Wait," I pulled the blanket even tighter, "did you . . . did you put this blanket on me last night?"

William looked at his boots again, like a little boy who had gotten caught doing something wrong. "You were drenched by the rain, appearing chilled. I trust my concern was not overly presumptuous."

Truth be told, I didn't know if it was. I had lost all sense of reality. "No, it's all right. Thank you."

"You're most welcome." He furrowed his thick gray brows. "A key. You employed a key to enter the dwelling. Whence did you procure such a key?"

Guilt flushed through my body, even though it shouldn't have. Legally, I had every right to be here.

"This house belongs to my husband, Joe. It's one of several properties he owns throughout the Northeast."

"You've mentioned a husband," he said. "Yet, no wedding band graces your hand."

"No, it doesn't," I said defensively, touching the pale area where my wedding band had been before I'd thrown it into the Hudson River the day before. "And I don't think it ever will again."

William made the gesture of an inhale, although no breath seemed to be entering his body. Was it just a force of habit? "'Tis a lovely pendant around your neck."

I reached up and rubbed it. "Thank you. It's a compass. Not a real one. A symbolic one. My father gave it to me. So that I would never feel lost."

William nodded and did another one of those fake inhales. "Well, then, Clara, er . . ." He paused. "You did not make mention of your surname."

I hesitated. "It's Kelly. Clara Kelly."

"Well, Clara Kelly, despite my earlier assertion, you are welcome to stay as long as you need." Then, without another word, he vanished right in front of me, leaving only faint footprints on the dusty floor.

Chapter 4

I would have thought the entire conversation was some sort of delusion—from dehydration or exhaustion—but there they were . . . William's footprints. Or *somebody's* footprints. Right there in front of me.

I stood there, not knowing what to do. How does one act after communicating with a ghost? Was it weird that I wanted him to come back? It had been a long time since I had a meaningful conversation with anyone. I had always been too afraid that I would let something slip about Joe and put my father in danger. I had gotten good at doing less talking and more listening. Surprisingly, no one seemed to notice. Most people liked to talk.

I looked at the doorway located next to the looking glass . . . er, mirror. (Seriously? After just one conversation with

a Civil War ghost and I was already using his vocabulary?)
I was eager to explore the rest of the house, and William
had given me his blessing. As much as I wanted to think of
myself as a rebel for having run away from my marriage, I was
still a rule follower at heart, and William's permission meant
something. After all, I had barged in here like I owned the
place.

The snuffed-out candle was still emitting wisps of smoke
as I walked toward the small twin bed that William had been
standing next to. It was covered with a crocheted blanket,
and I wondered about the person who made it. Had it been
William's wife? Mother? Daughter? William himself? Or
one of the humans who had lived in this house years later?
I sat on it, looking around the room, which had absolutely
no privacy because it was right next to the stairwell. Then I
stood and walked to the next room, a wide bedroom with
dusty stripwood flooring. In it, a bed was covered with plastic—also layered with dust. I carefully removed the plastic
and gently folded it. Underneath were reasonably clean bed-
sheets and a firm mattress. It didn't smell all that nice, but
this was certainly better than sleeping on a hard floor.

A closet was near the bed, and I opened its sliding door.
Empty wooden hangers swayed on a wooden bar. I stuck
my head in to see if anything else was inside (ghost moths,
perhaps?), but there wasn't anything but the faint smell of
cedar. I stuffed the dusty plastic I had pulled off the bed
inside and slid the door closed.

There was a window near a tall chest of drawers, and I peered down at the street. The roads and sidewalks were mostly empty, and sunlight was evaporating the puddles. My plan had been to check out downtown while I was here. I had always wanted to visit Salem. Joe never let me leave the hotel room when we traveled, and God forbid I go anywhere alone unless it was the gym, where his swole friends could watch me. "It's too dangerous," he would say, as if he were protecting me. Meanwhile, *he* was the one I needed protection from.

I stepped away from the window. No one seemed to be home next door, but I didn't want to risk being seen by someone who might be getting ready to go to work. It already felt like I was being watched.

Being watched.

I faced the bedroom.

"Are you still here?" I asked the air.

I flinched as William appeared suddenly near the closet. "Yes."

I took a breath. I didn't know if I was about to be rude, but I needed to say it. For my own sanity. "If I'm going to stay here a while, there are a few ground rules I would like to get out of the way, if that's okay."

"Ground rules?"

Probably an odd term to use with a ghost, who, at least according to the literature, had no need for a ground. Although, from my own short experience with them, ghosts used grounds, too. More proof you couldn't believe what you read. "Yes."

"All right," he said, intrigued.

"Okay . . . If this is going to work for the few days I'm going to stay here, I can't have you floating around invisible just watching me."

I could swear William turned a pale shade of red. "I am a decent man, Mrs. Kelly."

"It's Ms. Kelly."

"You mentioned a marriage, did you not?"

"In a legal sense, yes, I am married. But in every other way, no."

"But you are no longer a maiden."

Did I really want to be mansplained to by a ghost? "Let's move on, shall we? You can call me Clara, okay?"

William looked uncomfortable with the familiarity, but he nodded.

"Okay," I said, "so you're able to reveal yourself whenever you like?"

"So it seems."

"Well, I request that I'm given my privacy while I'm here. If I am in a room, I would like you to allow me to be in that room alone."

William seemed to be preoccupied by my jeans and T-shirt, and I suddenly wondered what a woman from 1863 might wear. If William had lived in this house through, say, the 1920s and 1960s, he had certainly gotten his share of skin-revealing flapper dresses and miniskirts. "Your seclusion holds value to you," he said.

"I didn't say seclusion. I said privacy. They are two different things." Seclusion, as in isolation, I had with Joe. *Lots* of it. Privacy, not so much. "My husband . . . well, he had video cameras in every room. Even the bathroom. Was always watching. Something was seriously wrong with him."

William stared at me, puzzled. "Video cameras?"

"Oh, um . . ." How to describe a camera? "A video camera is something you use when you want to watch someone or someplace when you're not there."

William furrowed his gray eyebrows.

"Okay, forget about that. What I'm asking is if I'm in a room that you would like to enter, could you . . . um, reveal yourself so that I know you're there? Like, knock or something? It's not like you need permission or anything. It's just so I know you want to come in."

William thought about it and nodded. "Yes, understood."

"Great." A wave of relief washed through me. "Thank you. I appreciate this, William."

"May we talk about my . . . *ground rules* as well?"

"Of course," I said, surprised. "I would like you to."

"If you'll excuse me for a moment . . ."

This time, William didn't disappear; he walked right through a door I hadn't seen that was on the same side of the bedroom as the closet.

I walked over and ran my hand along the door's edges. It was narrow and matched the wall decor, like a secret door. Although it had no knob, it clearly led somewhere. Could it be opened from the other side? I didn't have time to theorize because I heard some kind of lock shift, and the door opened with William holding a piece of paper—a *real* piece of paper—in his pale hand that he placed on a desk on the other side of the room. I picked it up.

"What is this?" I asked, examining the paper, which had brown edges, like it had been lying around for a while. My fingers traced the cursive handwriting.

"I taught myself how to use your writing implements."

"You mean ballpoint pens?"

He nodded.

There must have been a lot of time to kill over the years. The paper had a list of three items. "Did you write these just now?"

He nodded.

Were there speedwriting classes in the afterworld? Interesting. He was as concerned about my being here as I was about his. Enough to make a list. Before I could read William's list, he began speaking.

"Firstly, no callers are allowed beyond the primary dwelling quarters," he said.

"You mean there are other dwelling quarters? Besides the primary ones?"

He nodded and pointed through the narrow door with no doorknob. "That leads to another succession of chambers—three in number—and then to a staircase descending to a rear entryway. That entryway and this door are the sole means by which it is accessible."

That was a mouthful. "Fine." I was curious about this secret space, but I needed to respect William's wishes. Maybe the area had been for staff who lived in the house. Like maids or butlers. It was good to know, though, that there was another way to get into this place if I had to. Unless the backdoor also didn't have a doorknob. Was it for ghosts only now? I looked down at the next item on William's list.

"Secondly," William said, "nought shall be rearranged. The furnishings, whether exterior or within, are to abide in their present state."

"Don't worry. I don't plan on rearranging the furniture. I don't want to attract attention. If I don't see another person for the rest of my life, I would be okay with that."

"Be careful what you wish for," William said with a hint of sadness.

What had happened to William to make him so sad? Was it because he was alone or was there more to it? And why *was* he alone? I didn't want to ask. "But I am probably going to clean up a little. The dust is *killing* me. I mean . . . sorry, no offense."

"And," William continued, either ignoring me or giving me a little grace, "thirdly—"

"We treat one another with the utmost respect," I said, reading the words on the paper. "This is my favorite one." It had been a long time since a man I was living with was eager to respect my privacy and my wishes. Not since I lived with my dad.

"Very well," he said. "If these are amenable to you and that is all, may I take my leave?"

"You don't need to ask me for permission to come and go, William. This is your home. And I am your guest. Trust me, I lived a good portion of my life having to ask permission to do all kinds of things—and often being denied. I would never ask that of you. Or anyone. Thank you for letting me stay. And for treating me as . . . well, a person. I look forward to spending time with you for the next few days."

William searched my face. I wasn't sure for what. Sincerity? Deception? Then he nodded and vanished on the spot, instead of leaving by way of wall as he had done before. I wondered if there was some kind of method to his coming and going, or if it was simply dependent on his mood.

More sunlight was getting in through the windows now that the sun was higher in the sky, and I walked back to the staircase. When I got to the bottom level, I looked again at the floor. Still no footprints on the ground, mouse- or man-sized. Maybe William didn't spend much time down here.

I put the browned piece of paper with William's writing on the dining table and kept exploring. Another bathroom, smaller than a closet, was positioned under the stairs and across from the front door. Besides the kitchen to the right, that left only one other room I hadn't yet seen, located under the upstairs bedroom. As I entered, my breath hitched.

Books.

Hundreds of them.

Topped with years' worth of dust, but books nonetheless. The entire wall on the right side, below where the upstairs bedroom closet and strange door were located, was filled with shelves upon shelves of books. Many were leather-bound, but there were also some paperbacks and what looked like a stack of magazines in the bottom corner.

My eyes watered.

One of the hardest things about leaving Joe had been leaving behind my library, which was nothing like this, but I liked to think of it as a library anyway. Because Joe didn't like to read—didn't see the purpose of reading anything longer than a few Facebook posts on his phone—he didn't see the need to keep books out in the open. Or on a shelf or coffee table or bedroom nightstand. "They're eyesores," he said. "Dust collectors, too." He didn't even want to see me reading. If he did, he assumed I had nothing to do and would give me something to do. Like rearrange his sock drawer.

But I learned to choose my reading times carefully. The best times were after sex, when I knew Joe wouldn't wake for a couple of hours. I was pretty sure his problem with books had less to do with cleanliness and more to do with his insecurity. He figured that I thought reading made me better than him. (I totally did, but he didn't need to know that. Anyone who took the time to read books or try to understand the world from multiple perspectives got my respect.) I kept my dozen or so books—which were falling apart because of how many times I read them—under the bed and out of sight. They were worth more to me than any piece of jewelry Joe had ever bought me. Including my five-figure engagement ring. Which was now at the bottom of the Hudson.

I hurried over to the bookshelves and touched the leathery spines. *Adventures of Huckleberry Finn. The Great Gatsby. Romeo and Juliet.* Dozens of familiar titles and a few not so familiar, which sent a jolt of excitement through me. Nearby was a fireplace and a sofa covered with plastic, and next to one of the windows was a sturdy chair. I imagined myself sitting in this room over the next few days reading about all kinds of adventures—while plotting a few of my own.

My stomach let out a loud rumble.

First things first. I had to eat. When was the last time I put something in my stomach? Probably the banana and the bag of chips I bought before I got on the train to Salem. I needed to get some food in me and fast.

I hurried to my backpack, which was still lying on the floor in the entryway, and opened the pocket where I kept my money. Of the fifteen hundred dollars I had saved up for this little escapade, I was down to about a thousand. The burner phone and prepaid minutes had cost me a pretty penny, and train travel was ridiculously pricey these days. Ugh. Maybe it was a little shortsighted to toss my wedding band into the river. I could have pawned that baby. I had forgotten it had monetary value since it certainly didn't have any sentimental value for me. I imagined Joe laughing at my foolishness but quickly quieted my mind. *New life, remember?*

I took out about two hundred dollars and put the rest back. That should be enough to buy some nonperishables and supplies for a couple of days.

I grabbed some clean clothing and looked around the room. I was going to have to take William at his word that he would give me privacy. I quickly changed out of my still-damp clothing and put on a dry hoodie and a pair of jeans. I reached for the blond wig I had tossed on the floor and blew off the dust. In the pocket of my backpack was the hair dye I had bought at one of the drug stores near Penn Station in New York. I loved my red hair, but, unfortunately, so did Joe. I had heard him tell more than one person over the years that only 2 percent of the world's population had red hair and how proud he was to "have" one. Like he had captured a unicorn. With the water working in this old house, I would be able to dye my hair. That would keep him from finding me. And if he did manage to find me, would most certainly piss him off.

Things were looking up.

I took my burner phone and key and placed it in my back pocket and my money in my front pocket. I hesitated before opening the front door.

"William?" I said into the room.

I waited and wondered if William was counting Mississippis somewhere in his secret set of rooms so he didn't enter too quickly and look like he was spying on me. Or maybe he was just busy doing what ghosts do. Whatever that was. After a few moments, he revealed himself in the doorway that led to the room with the library.

"I'm going to step out and get some food." I had the urge to ask him if he needed anything, out of habit, but caught myself. "I'm guessing you don't happen to know if there is a supermarket nearby, do you?" The less time I spent dawdling outside, or looking lost, the better.

"Supermarket?"

"Well, maybe just a market."

"Old Ed's Farmer's Market lies just down the road a short distance," he said.

Something told me that old Ed was no longer around. "That's okay. I'll figure it out." I'd have to find a coffee shop with Wi-Fi somewhere, and I dreaded the thought. Coffee shops had people, and I needed to avoid people. For my sake. And theirs. Eventually, though, I'd have to find a place to charge my phone.

I glanced out the smudgy window at the house next door. What were the odds the old man had Wi-Fi and had disabled his password? Or had an easy one I could figure out like *password*.

"What might that be?" William asked, looking at my phone.

"Oh, this?" I held it out to him. "It's called a cell phone. You use it to . . . um . . . get information about things. And to call people."

"Call people?"

"People who are at far distances." I looked around the room. "Like that one there." An old rotary phone was sitting on a circular table between two of the front windows.

"At what distance are you able to communicate with others?"

"Very far. Like across the world." I hesitated. Was he interested in contacting someone from his time? His wife? Because that would be *really* far. I didn't think any service plan covered that.

He took a couple of steps toward me, intrigued by the tiny rectangle in my hands. With his gray, translucent skin and clothing, he looked so much like a person. And yet not. He was taller than I first thought, over six feet, for sure. I kept listening for a breath, but there was none, even though his chest was rising and falling. All I could hear was my own inhales and exhales.

"You must think me a buffoon," he said, examining the phone in my hand. "Not knowing of such things."

"No, not at all. Listen, we're all a product of when we lived—and *how* we've lived. I haven't lived very much in the past eight years. I'm sure other people would consider *me* a buffoon. But I'm going to change all that."

"You are exceedingly kind." He furrowed his brows, like he had something on his mind. "Might I offer to . . . accompany you?"

"You mean, outside? I thought you said you never left this house."

"I have not. Never had cause. Much like yourself, I haven't lived much, but maybe I can alter that circumstance, too."

I couldn't help but smile. "It is a kind offer, for sure. And I would love the pleasure of your company. But I hope you understand if I say no at this time. If I was a normal person, in a normal situation, maybe I would take you up on it. But I have been escorted just about everywhere for the past eight years, and I am looking forward to doing things by myself. The way I had always done them before."

I prayed I didn't hurt his feelings.

"But is that proper?" he asked, still concerned. "A lady traveling alone?"

"Yes, very much, William. Things have changed a lot since your day. And as far as women go, they have changed for the better. Which is what, I think, scared Joe so much. He felt like he was losing control and took it upon himself to control me." I caught myself. What was I doing? I must have had all this bottled up in me for so long that it needed to get out. "I'll be back soon."

I opened the front door and closed it behind me, tiptoeing a few steps toward the house next door. Making sure no one was around, I turned on the burner phone and checked the Wi-Fi networks and—*poof!*—there it was! A signal named WIGGINSWIRE.

Wiggins.

I looked at the doorbell.

The same name was listed there.

This had to be it.

I clicked on it and did a silent prayer that Wiggins wouldn't have a password—maybe for fear of forgetting it—and my prayers were answered. He didn't! The internet gods were with me today.

"Thank you, neighbor," I whispered and did a quick search for supermarkets near me. Then I put the phone back into my pocket, adjusted my wig, and hurried out of the driveway.

Chapter 5

Salem was lovely in the morning. Quiet. Peaceful. A small-town feel that was distinctly New England. Colonial-styled homes and dormered roofs, two to three stories. Brick facades on the main streets. Lots of signs for all kinds of tours—from historic to haunted—and psychic readings. A few tourists were strolling around, taking photos and sipping coffees. How I envied their idleness. Not having to worry about people seeing them. Or hurrying. Or looking over their shoulder. One day, I would get there.

Although there was no sign of Old Ed's Farmer's Market (what a shocker), Derby's Downtown Market was located only a few blocks away. Its big front windows were plastered with signs promoting various sales: steak tips and chicken drumsticks. As much as those sounded delightful, I needed to stick to mostly prepared foods and nonperishables for now. *Beef jerky, here I come!*

The market was already open. I pulled out a small shopping cart and walked quickly through the prepared foods section. My first item: a rotisserie chicken, which I planned to eat in its entirety the moment I got back to the house.

"Would you like to try some cold brew coffee, ma'am?" asked a young man, startling me.

He was standing at a small table that had tiny plastic cups filled halfway with a dark brown liquid. I glanced at his nametag, which read *Simon*.

"Sure," I said, my stomach grumbling at the mere mention of anything coffee related. I reached for a cup and threw it back like a shot of vodka. "Wow, this is *really* good," I said, glancing at one of the containers on the table. The brand name was Black Aye, which I had never heard of.

"Yes, this brand is only three ninety-nine, on sale, for a single serving, if you'd like to purchase." Simon, who still had sleep dust in the corners of his eyes, glanced at someone standing near the deli meats who was watching him intently. I figured it was a supervisor or maybe a representative from the coffee company.

Three ninety-nine didn't sound like much of a sale to me, but it was still cheaper than a cold brew from a coffee shop, and I didn't want the young man to seem like a bad salesperson.

"And this doesn't need refrigeration!" the young man added with a smile that was clearly put on for the person watching him.

Okay, I'll bite. "Really? No refrigeration?"

"This is shelf-stable cold brew."

I picked up one of the containers and pretended to read the label, since I already knew I was going to buy one. No refrigeration was a game changer. Clara was my name, and non-perishable was my game! "Okay, I'll take one."

"Great!" The young man glanced at his onlooker, who appeared satisfied and walked behind the deli counter. As soon as he did, Simon's smile disappeared, and his whole attitude changed. "Only three more miserable months," he said.

"Three more months?"

"Until I graduate and can tell that jerk of a boss I quit. Who needs this minimum-wage job?" He pulled out his phone from his pocket and began to scroll. "Take the coffee or don't take it. I really don't care."

I had a good mind to put the shelf-stable, total-ly-*not*-on-sale cold brew back on his little table, but at this point, my brain had gotten used to the idea of caffeine-induced stimulation, so I just nodded, put the coffee in my cart, and walked away. Why was I wasting time with Simon? I should have been halfway through the market already!

Rule #1: Don't talk to anyone else.

I hurried to the end of the aisle, picking up a few bananas and a bunch of grapes. Mission: to buy as little as I needed as cheaply as I could.

In the next aisle were paper plates and plastic forks. I thought about buying dish soap and a sponge to wash some of those plates and cups I had seen in one of the cabinets. Did it pay? I wasn't going to be in the house for very long. I put them in my cart anyway along with some plastic utensils. And a bar of soap. And toilet paper, tissues, and disinfectant wipes. *Sorry, environment.*

The baking aisle was next, and I nearly crashed into a young woman choosing between chocolate sprinkles and rainbow sprinkles. A very important choice, indeed. "Sorry, excuse me," I said, but she didn't hear me. She appeared lost in thought.

At the end of the aisle was a cheap-looking flashlight. I didn't know whose idea it was to place flashlights in the same aisle as baked goods, but bully for me! I scooped it up. Candlelight was for the birds. I looked at the package; the flashlight required D batteries, which were handily right on the next shelf. Things were looking up. As I looped around an endcap to go into the next aisle—dreaming of the cold brew channeling through my nervous system—I slammed into a shopping cart coming toward me.

"Oh, I'm so sorry!" I gushed. What was wrong with me? First, the sprinkles girl, and now some unsuspecting shopper whose face was blocked by an endcap of multipurpose flour.

As I carefully maneuvered my cart to take a look at my crash victim, I spotted the greenest eyes I'd ever seen, just above a pair of old baggy jeans and a flannel shirt.

"I'm fine," the green-eyed guy said. "No whiplash. No need to exchange driver's licenses and insurance cards." He smiled. "Here's a tip, though. If you don't want to develop a bad driving reputation here, you'd better follow the arrows." He pointed to the floor, indicating big white arrows that had been painted. I had clearly been going the wrong way the entire time I was in the store.

"Oh, I'm so sorry. I didn't realize. What's funny is that I'm generally a rule follower. I guess you have to know the rules before you can follow them." *Stop talking. For such a dutiful rule follower, you're breaking your first rule!*

"First time here?" he asked.

"Is it that obvious?"

"Maybe just a little." His smile made his green eyes sparkle.

Mayday. Mayday. Leave at once! "Well," I said. "I'd better go. Thanks for the tip."

I kept walking—the wrong way—down the aisle. To salvage this disastrous shopping trip, I needed to get out of there fast. At this rate, I would meet the entire town before I left the store.

I grabbed a few more things—including cookies, lots and lots of cookies—and made my way to one of the cashiers, a beady-eyed, middle-aged woman who looked like she was in a bad mood. Good. Maybe she wouldn't have the urge to talk to me.

As I placed my items on the conveyor belt, I could see Mr. Green Eyes, the guy I had crashed my shopping cart into, at the self-checkout with his items: a few scrub brushes, vinegar, and enough bottled water to quench the thirst of a Boy Scout troop. Not that I was being nosey. I ducked behind a display of candy until he paid and was walking out of the store.

"You got a store card, hon?" the cashier asked me. Her nametag read *Beverly*.

"Sorry, no."

"If you get one, you'll get the disinfectant wipes on sale."

"No, that's okay."

"Who doesn't want to save a dollar on disinfectant wipes?" she asked, astonished.

"I'm just passing through town," I said, which, unfortunately, seemed to pique her interest.

"Really? I can usually spot the tourists. You don't look like one. Where you from?"

"I'm sorry, but I'm in a rush."

"Are you saying I can't work and talk at the same time?" Beverly's over-plucked eyebrows raised up.

"No, no, it's just that—"

Two people began yelling a few registers down, getting Beverly's attention. And mine.

"Beckett Miller, you're a liar and, I told you, I never want to see you again!" One of the cashiers, a college-aged girl, was talking to a young man in a maroon Harvard University hoodie who was standing near her register.

"Maggie, I didn't do it," this Beckett Miller person was saying.

"Sure, the image miraculously sent itself." Maggie rolled her eyes. "You're going to get me in trouble. Go away."

"I'm here because you won't return my calls," Beckett Miller said.

"Sheesh, those two . . ." Beverly said, continuing to scan my items.

"You know them?"

"I know everyone around here, hon. 'Cept maybe you." She looked me up and down. "That's Officer Miller's boy. Smarty pants, he is, and he knows it. Too smart, if you ask me."

"Maggie!" Beckett Miller was imploring the young girl, but she finished with her customer and logged out of her register.

"I'm going on my break," Maggie said. "And you better leave, or I'm going to tell Devon to call the police. I want nothing to do with you."

"Fine!" Beckett said, but instead of leaving, he walked further into the store.

"Where do you think you're going?" this Maggie person said.

"Why should I tell you? You want nothing to do with me!"

"You got bags?" Beverly asked, startling me.

"No. I forgot them at home."

"I thought you were just passing through."

"I mean, I forgot them at home, where I live, and don't have any with me." I usually was a better liar than this. I had eight years of training. I was off my game.

"So you want paper bags then? Two?"

"Sure."

"They're five cents each. But that shouldn't be a problem for anyone who pays three ninety-nine for a single-serve of coffee." She held up the shelf-stable cold brew and looked at the label. "This stuff any good?"

"It's okay." I could feel myself losing patience with Beverly.

"All right then . . ." Beverly pressed a few buttons. "That'll be one-seventeen sixty-nine."

That much? Ugh. I handed her the money, and she gave me my change.

"Nice to see people pay with cash again. Never thought I'd see the day, but those credit card surcharges are no joke." Beverly handed me my receipt. "Have a nice day now."

"You too," I replied and hurried out the exit door.

Chapter 6

No sooner had I gotten to my front door and placed my groceries on the ground to reach for my key than my next-door neighbor opened his door. Our eyes met. Oh no. Too late. There was nowhere to hide.

"Well, hello!" said a cheery, wrinkly but clean-shaven face below a balding head where a few strands of white hair had been neatly combed. "How wonderful to see someone come out of this lovely house. I'm afraid since my Alma died, it's been very quiet around here. The name's Wiggins. Archie Wiggins."

Meeting neighbors was worse than talking to people at the market. I wasn't supposed to be leaving any sort of trace, and over the course of only a couple of hours, four people could provide a detailed description of me to a private detective. *Nice going.*

Mr. Wiggins was waiting for an answer, and because I couldn't think of anything else to say, I gave him one. "Clara. Clara Kelly."

"I'm sorry. Can you speak up?" He pointed to his left ear. "This darn ear hasn't been working too well for the past year or so. I guess my warranty ran out." He chuckled.

"My name is CLARA KELLY," I said loudly.

"Ah, Clara, happy to meet you." He looked behind me, into the house. "Do you live here with . . .?"

"Um . . . I don't really live here. My husband and I own this property. It's been in my husband's family for years, and it looks like we're going to sell, so I came to see what it looked like." I hoped that seemed plausible enough.

"Well, that's too bad. I thought we might become neighbors. I make an excellent chicken tortellini soup."

Mmmm, soup, my mind thought. I really needed to eat. "That would be nice. Maybe one day. I'm sorry, but—"

"My schedule is wide open. You know, the realtors have been trying to get me to sell this house for years." He pointed inside his doorway and shook his head. "Not interested."

I couldn't blame him. These old houses had such charm. Civil War ghost, notwithstanding. "From what I hear, there are all kinds of restrictions, too, when selling." I had heard Joe complain about them too many times to his realtor. "But if I lived here, I wouldn't want to leave."

"You and me both, young lady," Wiggins said when, suddenly, a car horn blared, the sound pinballing across the narrow driveway. Then a car drove past, its brakes screeching, followed by a loud bang.

"What on earth was that?!" Mr. Wiggins asked.

I hurried out of the driveway. An old-fashioned car, long and wide, was sitting in the middle of the street. A body was lying in front of it.

"Oh, my God, someone's been hit," I said and automatically reached for my phone to call 911, but then stopped. If I called the police, I would have to give my name. Giving my name might lead to questions. Questions might lead to answers. And answers were dangerous. For me.

"Is that Hazel Birchgirdle's car?" The old man hobbled next to me, appearing concerned. "Is she hurt?"

Ugh. The look on his face. It was a hundred times sadder than the saddest animal video I'd ever seen on social media. I turned on my burner phone and pressed 9-1-1, putting the phone to my ear. If I said it once, I said it a thousand times. Worst. Runaway. Ever.

Chapter 7

THE LOGO OF THE Salem Police Department was a silhouette of a witch flying on a broom. The city took this witch thing seriously. Meanwhile, I had the urge to call up the SPD public relations people and tell them they had it all wrong. They had a ghost population, not a witch population. Want proof? There was one living in my house. Who knew how many more there might be?

Mr. Wiggins had already gone to talk to the driver of the car, a woman who looked to be in her seventies like him. I knew Wiggins had mentioned the loss of a wife, but for a guy who had a bad ear and walking problems, he got over to Mrs. Birchgirdle pretty quickly. I detected a bit of a crush.

"I struggle to believe there are no more horses and carriages," said William, who suddenly appeared next to me.

"Are you crazy?" I asked. "What are you doing? Someone might see you."

He shook his head. "It is likely they cannot perceive my presence."

"How do you know that?"

"All those who have dwelt within my abode and strolled past my home through the passing years never were able to see me. Only you." He furrowed his brow. "Although, on one occasion, I gazed out the upper window, and a young lass, accompanied by her mother, passed by. She cast her eyes upward and, lo and behold, she spied me and offered a friendly wave. She, too, beheld my presence."

"How did you know I would be able to see you?"

William shrugged. "I was unaware that you could perceive me, Clara. Hence, I pressed my heels upon the floor, hoping to beckon you upstairs. It was not until you uttered a cry of alarm at the sight of me that I was assured of your awareness."

"You mean you tricked me?"

"Nay," he said, crossing his arms, "I merely directed your path."

Hmmm . . . was gaslighting a thing in the late 1800s? "So," I asked, "how does it work? Why can only some people see you?"

"I know not."

A tall, buff police officer was talking with Wiggins, who turned and pointed toward me. *No, no, no. I can't get in-*

volved. It was bad enough I placed the call to 911 and had to give my name.

Sure enough, the officer began walking toward me. I covered my mouth, pretending I had to sneeze, and whispered to William. "I can't talk to you. People will think I'm crazy. You need to go."

William didn't move.

"William, you need to go."

What if this police officer was one of those people who could see William? Was I supposed to introduce him? Or pretend there was nothing to see here?

"Hello, officer," I said, taking my hand from my mouth when he was close by. "How can I help you?"

"I'm Officer Callahan, Salem Police Department." He motioned toward the scene of the accident. "Archie Wiggins said the two of you were chatting when the accident happened. Is that right?"

"The two of *us*?" I asked, panicked. Was he talking about William and me? I stood there waiting for Officer Callahan to notice William, who was staring right at him, scrutinizing him like he was a lab experiment. But Callahan didn't. William was right. He couldn't see him. Meanwhile, Officer Callahan was looking at me expectantly.

"Yes, I'm sorry," I coughed. "Mr. Wiggins and me, right . . . We were standing right over there." I pointed to the driveway and pierced William right through the stomach with my finger. He seemed unbothered, but I quickly pulled my hand back in horror.

"Is something the matter?" Officer Callahan asked, glancing at my arm.

"Oh, nothing. It's just that . . ." I did small rotations with my arm. "My shoulder is sore. You know, the gym." *Is that the best you can do?* "We didn't see anything. Mr. Wiggins and me, I mean. We just heard a crash."

"Yes, Mr. Wiggins told me. Your name is Clara Kelly? You called in the accident?"

So much for anonymity. "Yes, that is correct."

"And you live . . ." He looked at the house.

"I don't live here. Well, sort of, I do. The house belongs to my husband, Joseph Turner. It's been in his family for generations and he's been wanting to sell. I'm here taking a look, trying to get the place in order." My own version of two truths and a lie.

Officer Callahan raised his neatly trimmed eyebrows on his tanned face. He must have been accustomed to wearing sunglasses because he had white raccoon eyes. "Well, you'll get a pretty penny. A lot of interest in Salem these days. Fortunately, and unfortunately. A lot of us who live here try to keep the small-town feel." He held up a notepad. "Can I have your address in . . ."

"New York," I said, even though I didn't want to. But I was raised never to lie to a police officer. I might as well have had my hand on a Bible and been standing on a witness stand. I gave him the rest of my address.

"Thank you. I already have your phone number. I'll be in touch if I need anything."

Great.

He turned to go but stopped. "Can you do me a favor?"

"Um, sure."

"I don't know how long you're staying, but if you could keep an eye on Mr. Wiggins. He hasn't been feeling too well lately. And Mrs. Birchgirdle is going to need some support as well."

"Of course," I said before I could keep the words from coming out of my mouth.

"From what I understand, it wasn't her fault. An eyewitness said Beckett just walked right in front of her car, didn't even hear the horn."

"Wait, did you say Beckett?" I glanced over at the body in front of Mrs. Birchgirdle's car. An officer was covering it with a black tarp, but before he did, I could see the maroon hoodie on the torso.

"Yeah, you know him?" Officer Callahan asked.

"No, not really. But I think I saw him this morning at the market."

"Really?" Callahan wrote something down on his pad. "What did you see?"

I saw him in a shouting match with a young woman. Don't get involved. Don't get involved. "Not much, really. Just him talking to one of the cashiers."

"He was a bit troubled, that kid." Officer Callahan took a long breath. "I know the family. His father is a colleague of mine. This is going to devastate him. As I said, we're a small, tight-knit group around here. The world may know Salem as a tourist attraction. But to us it's home." He flipped his notepad closed. "I'll be in touch, Mrs. Kelly."

I had the urge to shout "Ms." as Officer Callahan walked back toward the scene of the accident. He stopped briefly to talk to Mr. Wiggins, who was gently guiding Mrs. Birchgirdle toward me. The poor thing looked shaken up. She was leaning on Wiggins's chubby frame as an ambulance arrived, tears streaming from her eyes.

"Come right this way, Hazel," Mr. Wiggins was saying. "I'll make you a cup of tea."

"Why didn't he move out of the way?" she asked as she passed me. "I beeped my horn."

And that horn was *loud*. I think I would have heard it if I were still in New York.

"Now, now, Hazel," Mr. Wiggins said. "Officer Callahan said Beckett was wearing earbuds or whatever they're called. He didn't hear you. It's not your fault."

"If only my reflexes had been better. You know my Selena is always telling me I shouldn't be driving. Oh, Archie, they're going to take away my car. Poor Beckett. I feel just awful."

"Let's not worry about that now." Mr. Wiggins looked at me. "I'm going to take Hazel inside for a bit. It was very nice to meet you, Clara."

"Of course. Please let me know if you need anything."

"What are these earbuds he speaks of?" William asked me when Mr. Wiggins and Mrs. Birchgirdle had entered the house. I had totally forgotten he was standing there.

"They're these things we can put in our ears and listen to music."

"Like a Walkman?"

I looked at him in surprise. "You know what a Walkman is?"

"One of the young ones who resided in my dwelling possessed such a contrivance. It was marked as such on its side. She would recline in bed with it upon her ears."

"Yes, earbuds are similar," I said.

He searched my face. "What ails you? Your countenance bears a pensive visage."

"Nothing," I lied, now self-conscious about my pensive visage. My mind was playing back the scene at the market between Beckett and the cashier, Maggie. Maybe the whole incident had made Beckett so distraught that he was totally in his head and not able to detect Mrs. Birchgirdle's car when he was crossing the street.

"We'd better go," I said.

"We?"

"Yes, the two of us. Nothing good can come from us standing out here."

More onlookers were gathering near the scene of the accident, where police barricades were placed to help the EMTs have access to the body and not have to deal with all the bystanders. I touched my wig to make sure my red hair was properly hidden. Meanwhile, William was looking around. At the buildings. At the people. At everything.

"Why do you don that?" He motioned to my wig.

"I'm trying to hide."

"Not very well."

"No kidding, and you're not helping. C'mon, we need to go."

He nodded and, before I could say another word, disappeared on the spot.

I looked around to see if anyone was looking at me and wondering why a woman who was wearing an obvious wig was talking to herself, but everyone seemed preoccupied with the accident. I walked quickly back to the house, replaying the movie reel of Beckett Miller and the cashier in my mind. *It's not your problem*, I told myself. I had other problems to contend with. I managed to clear Beckett Miller out of my mind. But then I saw him again.

Standing on my doorstep.

Chapter 8

"You have to help me," Beckett said, his maroon Harvard hoodie now a dark shade of gray.

You've got to be kidding me. Not another one. Out of all the people assembling here, was I the only one lucky enough to see ghosts? What about Callahan or Birchgirdle or any one of the dozens of looky-loos gawking at the body?

Move on, new spirit. Go haunt someone else.

I pretended not to see him. I began whistling and humming a happy tune, looking up at the blue sky and the puffy clouds, but he was having none of it.

"Listen to me," he said, blocking my way.

I was working up the nerve to walk right through him—judging by the way my finger tore through William's torso, I could apparently do that—but he reached out and put his hand on my arm.

I pulled back. What the heck? I *felt* that. Felt *him*. How could that be? "Hey!"

"I *knew* it! I knew you could see me," Beckett said.

"And why is that?"

"I saw you talking to *him*." He pointed inside the house where William was probably planning a tour of Salem now that he had ventured outside for the first time in a hundred fifty years. "Who's the guy in the old-timey military getup anyway?"

Beckett was practically shouting, and out of habit, I shushed him, looking toward Mr. Wiggins's house. Of course, Wiggins probably couldn't hear Beckett. Even with his good ear. But the last thing I wanted was for him to open his door and see me talking to a ghost—or to myself—in our shared driveway. I stepped inside my house. "You need to leave."

I was about to close the door when Beckett's ghost said, "I can't."

"And why is that?"

"Because I was murdered."

"Excuse me?"

"I said *murdered*!" he shouted.

"Really? Did you see Mrs. Birchgirdle? I don't know her, but she seems devastated by what happened. You're telling me that was all an act? That she saw you coming and thought, well, why not, and mowed you down in the middle of the street?"

Beckett shook his head. "No, Mrs. Birchgirdle is a nice lady. My family has known her for years. She wouldn't hurt a fly. Someone else murdered me, I know it."

"I don't believe you," I said, even though I wasn't sure if I didn't.

"Why not?"

"Oh, I don't know. Because I saw you at the market today. It was hard *not* to see you. You certainly were making a scene. And the cashier you were arguing with called you a liar."

"Yeah, well, you don't know the whole story." Beckett crossed his arms.

"Good, because I don't want to know." I reached for the door. I don't know why I felt the need to close it. William certainly had no trouble walking through walls.

"Wait, you have to listen." Beckett tried to slip into the house, but it was like he was walking into glass. He couldn't cross the threshold.

"What's the matter?" I asked.

"I don't know. I can't seem to come in."

"You must extend an invitation for him to enter." William was suddenly standing next to me, eyeing Beckett. "You or I, I mean."

"I have to invite him in?" I asked. "Like a vampire?"

"I don't believe in those," Beckett said.

"Yeah, well, until this morning, I didn't believe in ghosts either," I said. "Listen, I can't help you, Beckett. That's your name, right? Why don't you go talk to Officer Callahan?"

"I tried to get his attention, but he can't see me. Nobody can but you."

I looked at William, who was giving me an *I told you so* face.

Beckett appeared exasperated. "Listen, somebody killed me. And I have no idea who you are, but it seems like you're the only person who can help me."

"I'm sorry. I have my own problems," I said, but then I had a thought. "Maybe you can go find your family. You won't have to be invited in there, right? Because you live there. And maybe they can see you."

Beckett considered this. "That's not a bad idea. Good thinking. I'll give it a try." He was about to walk away but stopped. "Oh, one more thing," he said. "When you see Mrs. Birchgirdle . . . Please let her know the accident wasn't her fault."

"Okay. Whatever. Thanks. Good luck."

I quickly shut the door and turned to face William. "Is there anything else you need to tell me?" I took the two bags I had placed on the floor, moved them to the dining table, and began unpacking the groceries.

"What do you mean?" William asked.

"Well, apparently you *can* go outside, even though you *haven't* gone outside, and then I find out that other people can see you besides me."

"As I did convey, only a select few."

"Oh, goody. And I also find out that there are other ghosts."

"There do exist other ghosts."

"Yes, I know that now."

"A few have glimpsed me through the windows over the passing years. They endeavored to gain entry, and I discerned they could not unless I extended an invitation."

"Did you?"

"On occasion. They informed me that their demise occurred under mysterious circumstances. Alas, I, being of spectral nature, could offer them no aid." He paused. "What else do you wish to inquire about?"

Lots. "So, every time a person dies, they just float around haunting people?"

"No, most ghosts pass on."

"To where?" Now that William opened the door to religion, I was ready to go right through.

"I am uncertain."

"But why are some still here? Why is Beckett here?"

"My understanding is there exists an unresolved matter, a mysterious circumstance. Those who linger upon the earthly realm after departing, it seems their souls find no solace, so they are unable to rest."

I stopped unpacking the bags. Did that mean what Beckett said was true? That he had been murdered? I looked at William. And did that mean William was here because there had been some mysterious circumstances associated with *his* death?

"Is there aught else you wish to inquire?" William asked.

"Why was I able to feel Beckett when he touched me?"

"Pardon me?"

"His arm went through me like I expected it to, but I could *feel* him. Just a little."

"I am uncertain. I have never laid my hands upon a human before. Not even my human wife."

"You had a wife?"

"Yes."

"She lived here?"

"Yes. Long ago."

"What happened to her?"

William looked uncomfortable again. "Due to the manner of my demise, there were few suitors who sought her hand. Eventually, she wedded George Bell, the village blacksmith. Alas, he proved not to be very kind."

I found myself pulling out one of the dusty dining room chairs and sitting down, riveted. Nature of his death? Having to haunt a home inhabited by his wife and another man? This was better than Netflix. "You lived here and watched your wife and this George person?"

"There was naught I could accomplish. I endeavored to reveal my presence, but Flora was unable to perceive or sense me."

"But why? I could feel Beckett."

"You could also *see* him," William said. "Perhaps the two are connected. And I had not learned yet to manipulate objects."

Wow. Trapped in a house with an unkind man. Unable to communicate. I felt seen. "I'm so sorry. That must have been awful."

"My actions, it seems, have stained this house. And my descendants. It grew difficult to witness the fate of my progeny, their offspring, and the generations that followed. I merely kept to myself after some time."

"Wait a minute." I started doing the math. The house had been in Joe's family for generations. "If what you're saying is true, that means that . . ."

William nodded. "Yes, your husband, Joe."

Could it be? William was Joe's great-great-great-great-grandfather. Or something like that. "Wait, you think something you did has cursed this house?" I asked.

"Yes, in so many words."

"That's not true."

William shook his head. "As you said before, you don't know me."

"What I mean is, we're all responsible for our own actions. I don't know what you did . . ." I paused in case William had the urge to tell me. He didn't. "But that can't have an effect on how your great-great-great-great-grandson behaves."

"How can you be certain?"

"Well, I'm not, really. But they're finding out more and more in science that we are in control of our destiny. What happens to us has more to do with our behavior than the genes we have been dealt."

"Destiny?" William appeared lost.

"But that's beside the point. You've been in this house, keeping to yourself, for more than a hundred and fifty years, blaming yourself for what happened to your family?"

"I'd like to append the established ground rules now." William raised the browned piece of paper I had placed on the dining room table.

"Wait, like, see that?" I said. "You're able to hold something in your hand. You're able to make footprints on the ground when you want to. Why can't Beckett just knock off Officer Callahan's hat or scribble *I was murdered* on a piece of paper and put it on Officer Callahan's windshield?"

"It is when we undertake an action with intention that we are able to cross realms." William disappeared, placed the paper back on the table, and suddenly the package of beef jerky I had set on the table flew up into the air. He reappeared holding it. "But this skill does not present right away. It takes time and diligent effort to master this."

I motioned to the piece of paper he had placed on the table. "How long did it take you to learn to use a ballpoint pen?"

"A considerable span of time, I reckon. The smaller the object, the greater the need for practice."

I picked up the piece of paper. "You said you wanted to add something to the ground rules?"

"Yes." He adjusted his military jacket. "I'd like to add that we don't talk about the past."

I searched his pale blue eyes. I had a burning desire to know what had happened to William Kensington, and yet I, too, had a burning desire to leave behind my past. "Agreed," I said. "I'll add it to the list."

"Very well," William said and disappeared again.

A sadness came over me as I placed the paper on the table. I had agreed to William's terms, but I hoped the matter wasn't settled. William had to know that he had nothing to do with whatever happened to his descendants. Maybe I could convince him of that.

My stomach grumbled.

But if I didn't get some food in me soon, I wouldn't be of any help to anyone.

Chapter 9

Sleep eluded me. Even after spending the rest of the afternoon cleaning up as much dust as my eyes and nose could tolerate and working up a proper exhaustion. I couldn't stop thinking about three things: 1) how long it took for a person to starve to death—I had been naïve to think fifteen hundred dollars would get me far, 2) what William Kensington had done that could be so bad, and 3) if Beckett Miller was able to find someone else to help him.

I was more than overjoyed that Beckett was unable to come into the house unless invited. I wouldn't have to deal with him floating over my bed and singing the lyrics to "I'm Henry the Eighth, I Am" like Patrick Swayze in *Ghost*. But if what William said was right, something was keeping Beckett from crossing over. And William, too. And as much as I didn't want to admit it, I cared about what happened to people—*and* ghosts, apparently. They were people, too.

I got out of bed and carefully navigated toward the staircase, thankful for the streetlights in front of the house, which let in enough light for me to get around now that I knew where I was going. When I got to the staircase, I reached for the flashlight, filled with fresh batteries that I had picked up at the market. No more Wee Willie Winkie for me! I walked down the stairs.

I did a quick scan of the floor for more tiny footprints and thought I saw a few by the front windows. I should have picked up a mousetrap at the market. On the table was the six-pack of seltzer I had purchased. I opened a can and guzzled it. Maybe I couldn't sleep because I was hungry. I thought about having some more beef jerky, but I already had way more salt than any one person should have in a day.

I glanced at the newspaper I had picked up on the way home from the market, just in case my disappearance had somehow made the news (unsurprisingly, it didn't), when I heard a noise. It was coming from outside.

Strangely, my first thought wasn't Joe, which I considered a victory in itself. It was Beckett. Maybe he was still hanging around out there trying to get my attention.

Yawp!

There it was again. But it didn't sound like a person. Or even a ghost person. More like some kind of animal. Was

Beckett trying to fool me into opening the door? *Get a grip.* Even if he was, as long as I didn't invite him in, I was good.

I slowly turned the deadbolt of the front door and then the doorknob. As the door creaked open, I peered outside.

No one was there, and the streetlight was allowing me to see a good portion of the driveway.

Yawp!

I turned my head. The noise was coming from the back of the driveway, which looked like it had once been a garden, but was now just mud and fallen branches. Lots of them. Probably just a mouse.

Yawp!

Ugh. It didn't sound like a mouse. It sounded like something larger, and also like something in trouble. I wanted to forget about the noise, go inside, get back under the dusty covers upstairs, and try to fall asleep, but I knew it was hopeless. All I'd be able to think about was that I hadn't helped whatever it was. I put on my boots lying by the door, reached for the flashlight, grabbed the key, in case I accidentally got locked out, because the way my luck was going I probably would, and headed outside.

The mud was squishy from the recent rain, and my shoes sank about an inch with each step, soaking my feet. *Why was I out here again?*

Yawp!

Oh, yeah, that was why. I shined my flashlight all around, but didn't see anything. Nothing was moving.

Yawp!

There. In the back. By some kind of pipe. The sound was coming from there.

Yawp!

Yep, it definitely was. From *inside* the pipe. With my luck, it would be a great big rat. Or a possum—I knew those things were harmless, but they gave me the creeps.

I carefully walked over, crept down, and shined my flashlight into the pipe. Sure enough, two tiny eyes peered back at me, surrounded by dirty, whitish hair. Was that a dog?

Yawp!

Yes, it was a dog. A little fur ball of an animal. The poor thing was stuck.

"How did you get in there?" I asked.

The dog started whimpering, getting excited at the sight of me, and was trying to move, but looked like it was falling farther back. The little thing was lucky the pipe wasn't facing up, or else it would have filled with water from the rain, and it might have drowned. Where did this pipe lead? If the dog went back any farther, I'd never be able to get him.

"Don't worry, fella. Relax. I'll help you."

Bark!

Weird. It was like the dog knew what I was saying. And the bark was loud, echoing through the pipe. I glanced at Mr. Wiggins's house. I hoped he slept with his bad ear toward the driveway.

I positioned my flashlight so that it was shining inside the pipe and reached in with my hand. "Please don't bite me."

When my hand got far enough, the dog began licking it desperately. I felt around its furry head for something to hold on to, like a collar, but there was none. The dog continued to squirm—so much so, it was pushing itself back, and I couldn't reach it anymore.

"Wait, wait!" I said into the pipe. "Don't do that! Relax."

"What's going on?"

Beckett's voice startled me, and I knocked the flashlight into the mud. I picked it up, wiped the dirt from the beam, and shined it all around, but I didn't see him.

"Don't do that!" I said. "You scared me."

"You look different." Beckett was studying my hair, and I realized I had left my blond wig in the house. "What are you doing?" he asked.

"There's a dog stuck in this pipe, and I'm trying to help it. Where are you?" I shined my light toward the street and found Beckett's head. It looked disembodied. "What are you doing here?"

"My parents couldn't see me. They looked so sad. I was shouting at the top of my lungs, but they couldn't hear me either. I tried to move things—chairs, tables, lamps. I couldn't."

"I know. You have to learn to do those things. Concentrate really, really hard, especially with small stuff like pens and pencils. You need to focus. Have intention. It takes practice. Years of practice, I think."

"I don't have years. The murderer will get away with it if we let too much time lapse. Wait . . . how do you know so much about being a ghost anyway?"

"I don't. But I live with one. I mean, I'm staying with one. Temporarily. One who has been around a long time."

Beckett came closer. "You're the only one who can help me. Or him. One of you has to."

"Listen, Beckett, I'm sorry for what's happened to you. I really am. But I just can't—"

Yawp!

I shined my flashlight into the pipe. The dog was even farther back than he was a few seconds ago. "Don't move, little one," I said into the pipe.

"Hey, I know . . ." Beckett glanced at the pipe. "If you help me, I'll help you free the dog."

"What are you talking about? You couldn't even get the attention of your parents. How are you going to free this dog?"

"I'll focus, like you said. Have . . . you know, intention."

I shined my flashlight at the poor thing in the pipe. The dog was just sitting in there, waiting. Trusting that I had some sort of plan. But there was no way I wanted to be indebted to a paranoid ghost. But, wait, I didn't need Beckett!

"William," I whispered. "William, are you there?" I shined my flashlight toward the house, but nothing happened.

"He's probably busy," Beckett said.

I tried to get up, when Beckett said, "And by the time you go and find him, this poor dog might fall so far back, he'll end up in the sewer."

"This leads to the sewer?" I asked, terrified.

"It might."

Ugh. "All right. Can you try to push the dog from the other side? And I'll reach in and—"

"Only if you help me."

I shined my flashlight on Beckett. "Are you serious? You would let this little dog die if I don't help you?"

"What do I care about a little dog?"

I had a feeling the cashier was right. This guy really *was* a jerk. "So, why should I care about *you*?"

"You don't have to. You care about the dog." He smirked.

"You know, you don't know me too well. I don't respond well to extortion."

Yawp!

I shined my light inside the pipe again, and the little dog was clawing at the pipe and going backward again. "Don't do that," I whispered. "Be still just a little longer."

"You're wasting time, Ghost Whisperer," Beckett said. "Do we have a deal?"

"How do you expect me to help you? I'm not a private detective."

"All I ask is that you do a little snooping. Find out what you can. I'll help you along the way."

"Is you helping supposed to motivate me?" I got down on my knees in the mud. The dog was about a foot farther away than it was before. "How do I even know you're telling the truth? That you can do this?"

"I guess you'll have to trust me."

"You don't know what you're asking of me." Helping Beckett meant showing my face to more people of Salem. It meant wasting time when I should be plotting my next safe house and my next route. Plotting the rest of my life!

"Time's a-ticking." Beckett pointed to his ghost watch on his ghost wrist.

Yawp!

"Fine," I said, shining the light back up into Beckett's face. "Now, help this dog."

Beckett disappeared instantly, and I shined the flashlight back into the pipe.

"Hold on, doggie. Help is on the way. It's going to be okay."

I waited. A minute passed and maybe another. What was taking so long? The dog started whimpering and clawing again.

"Where are you?" I whispered into the pipe.

"If you think it's so easy, you do it," Beckett said from somewhere on the other side of the pipe, in the dark.

"Just concentrate," I said. "Do what you did before when you tried to grab me. Focus on one spot."

"It's not working," he said.

"Just imagine that person who murdered you getting away with it. What would you want to do to that person?"

Suddenly, the dog let out a tiny squeak, and it moved forward slightly. Like it was being shoved from behind, its little paws clawing at the sides of the pipe. It was working.

"That's it. That's it. You got it. Just one more push. Do it again."

"I don't even know how I did that," Beckett said.

"Well, do everything you did again. Close your eyes. Focus on the murderer."

Another tiny yelp, and the dog inched forward.

"Again!" I said to Beckett.

After a few more nudges, I put the flashlight down and reached into the pipe with both hands. I could feel the dog's head, and my fingers got wet. The dog was licking me again.

"Wait, little one, I know. Hold on." I wedged my fingers behind the dog's head and gently pulled forward. Slowly, the dog's body came toward me until I was able to pull it all the way out.

"Ugh, you smell disgusting," I said, plopping the hairy mess onto my lap. The dog began spinning round and round, trying to lick my face. I giggled. "You're welcome."

"Don't forget. We have a deal." Beckett's ghost arm gave me a thumbs-up in the beam of the flashlight.

"Yeah, I know. Thank you for doing this."

"No problem. Get a good night's sleep now. You'll need it tomorrow," he said, his arm disappearing.

I picked up the flashlight and shined it on the dog. "Boy, are you a mess. Where do you live?" I searched for a collar, but there was none. At least I couldn't find one in the dog's too-long, too-filthy matted hair. If this was someone's dog, it had been a long time since the poor thing had been cared for.

"Let's get out of here." I tried to stand, but my hands sunk deeper in the mud. "You know, if *you* look this bad," I said to the dog. "I could only imagine what *I* look like."

I managed to get up, and as I carried the dog and the flashlight toward the door, I was surprised to find it already open and William standing there, barely visible in the dim streetlight.

"You look a fright," he said, stepping back as I walked in.

"Where *were* you? I was calling for you," I said, sounding all whiny. I closed the door.

"What, pray tell, is that?" He stared at the animal in my hands.

"It's a dog. And we're both about to take what will probably be the coldest bath on record."

Chapter 10

When I came back downstairs with the dog in my hands, both of us were shivering. I had managed to get most of the mud off me because it was mainly on my clothing, but the poor dog had so much hair, it was impossible to get all the dirt off without submerging the tiny thing into the cold water, and the dog hair absorbed it like a sponge.

The moment my foot touched the downstairs flooring, I sensed something was different in the house.

Heat.

The rooms were much warmer than before.

What now? Is the house on fire?

I hurried into the living room. A fire was roaring in the fireplace, and William was standing before it.

"Did you do this?" I asked, although it was obvious he had.

"Is that all right?" William said. "My apologies for my unavailability when you required assistance. I had embarked on a stroll. My first in many years."

"Please. I was being rude. No apologies needed."

I sat down on the little rug in front of the fireplace and placed the dog in my lap. He did a quick circle before getting comfortable right on top of me.

"I didn't know the fireplace worked," I said. "Where did you get the wood?"

"At the back of the dwelling." He pointed to the elusive—and mostly inaccessible—back rooms of the house. "'Tis remarkably dry. A trifle smoky, though. I suspect a potential obstruction." He pointed up the chimney. "Yet the majority of the smoke appears to ascend."

"It's fine. Thank you."

William was eyeing the dog warily, but the dog's droopy eyes were watching William, unfazed.

"He doesn't seem to mind you," I said. "No barking or anything."

"He?" William asked.

"I found out during bath time that our little friend is a boy."

"What is his name?"

"I don't know. And I don't want to know. No attachments."

"Whence does he hail?"

"I don't know. But he can't stay here."

Another thing I had to do. In addition to rearranging my life, I had to find shelter for a dog. Oh, and if that weren't enough, I had to find a so-called murderer for a person I wasn't even sure was murdered. And whom I didn't like at all.

"Well, good night," William said.

"Good night, William. And thank you for this." I motioned toward the fire.

As William disappeared, I rubbed the belly of the dog. If you could call it a belly. Underneath all that still-damp hair, there was mostly bone. The dog hadn't eaten well in a long time. I placed him on the floor. "I'll be right back."

I walked out of the room and immediately wanted to walk back in. It was so toasty warm in there. But I hurried into the kitchen and picked up the flashlight, which was still caked with mud. I flicked it on and opened one of the kitchen cabinets, pulling down an old bowl and wiping it with a disinfectant wipe. I was about to walk toward the dining room table, where all that was left of the rotisserie chicken were two wings, when I nearly tripped over the dog.

"What are you doing in here, boy?"

He just looked up at me.

"Are you hungry? I bet you are." I scraped as much meat as I could off the wings and placed it all in the bowl, which I put on the floor, shining a light on it. Before I could say *bon apetit*, the dog licked the bowl clean. I scraped whatever more I could from the chicken, which wasn't much, and barely placed it in the bowl before the dog gobbled it up. I got another bowl and poured some water into it, placing it next to the other.

"Voilà!"

Then I placed two pieces of newspaper on the floor near the front door, moving my muddy boots to the side.

"I can't walk you, boy. So this will have to do."

The dog took more than a dozen laps of the water and then walked right over to the newspaper.

"Well, would you look at that," I said. "This dog stuff is easier than I thought."

He sniffed every inch of the paper before stepping off it and peeing in the corner of the room on the wood floor.

"Um, we'll have to work on that," I said. "I mean, your owner will have to work on that."

I grabbed the flashlight and the rest of the blankets piled up near the front door and brought them into the living room, making a quick bed for the dog in front of the fireplace. Then I peeled the plastic off a corner of the sofa and pressed down on the cushion. *Not bad.* I folded one of the blankets in a square for a pillow and placed it down, and wrapped the last blanket around myself.

The dog came in, bypassed the bed I made for him, and hurried toward the sofa where I was sitting. He lifted his front paws onto the cushion.

"That's your bed over there." I pointed.

Bark!

"Over there," I emphasized. He gazed up at me with his big, sleepy eyes, looking pretty pitiful with all that still-wet matted hair. He had been on his own much longer than I had.

"Oh, all right."

I scooped him up and put him onto the sofa next to me. He climbed onto me and spun several times before settling himself onto my lap. I stroked his little head.

"Make yourself at home . . ." *What was I going to call him?* What I said to William had been true; I didn't need any attachments. Life on the road was hard enough. But everyone needed a name. Even if it wasn't a real name. "Well, since you're a boy, I'll call you Boy until you find your forever home. All right?"

That seemed to be okay with Boy, who barely opened his eyes to acknowledge the moniker.

I leaned back against the sofa. How was I supposed to find Boy a home looking like this? Would his owners even recognize him? Did he have owners? I would have to find a groomer before I did anything else. And how much was that going to cost me?

Joe entered my mind. I could hear him thundering on and on about my "frivolous purchases," like the time I had bought my father front-row concert tickets to see Earth, Wind & Fire, his favorite band. My father talked about that concert until his dying day. I smiled. Now I had to spend who knows how much to groom a dog that I wasn't going to keep. Maybe Joe was right. I stunk at money management. Because with the way my money was going—my fingers traced Boy's skeletal tummy—pretty soon I would be skin and bones, too.

Chapter 11

ACCORDING TO THE INTERNET I pilfered from Mr. Wiggins, The Pampered Pup was located only a few blocks past Derby's Downtown Market. It seemed that most of Salem was grouped into a convenient downtown, and if you got out early enough, you didn't run into too many tourists.

I held Boy in my hands as I peered into The Pampered Pup's large windows. There wasn't much to see. Just an open area in the front with a closed off section behind a register that was accessible via a little gate, and then swinging doors that led to a back area, where, presumably, pups were pampered.

I opened the door, setting off a little bell.

"I'll be right there!" said a male voice from the back room.

"Don't be afraid. It's going to be all right," I said to Boy, even though he seemed perfectly content in my arms. I was clearly projecting my feelings onto him. But he didn't seem to mind. He was preoccupied with my blond wig, which I had to snatch from him that morning as he ran playfully throughout the house, kicking up dust.

As the doors that led to the back area swung open, I was greeted by the second greenest pair of eyes I had ever seen. And, surprisingly, they belonged to the same person who owned the first.

"Hey, it's you," said the guy whose cart I had slammed into at Derby's market.

"You work here?" I asked.

"Kind of. I own the place."

"Really?"

"You seem surprised."

"Well, no, I just didn't expect to see you again."

"Sorry to disappoint you."

"No, that's not—"

"I know. I'm just kidding. I'm Sebastian." He smiled, but when he looked at Boy in my arms, his face changed.

"He isn't mine," I said quickly before he reported me for animal abuse. "Do you know of anyone who reported a missing dog?"

"No, I'm afraid I don't. But you may want to check with the town shelter. A few blocks from here. Where did you find him?"

"In my yard. He was stuck in a pipe."

"How terrible." Sebastian opened the little gate and stepped into the main area. He reached out and petted Boy, who tried desperately to lick his hand.

"He likes you," I said.

"He had to be on his own for a long time to get this way. It's a boy?"

I nodded.

"What's his name?"

"He didn't have a collar, but . . . well, I named him Boy."

"Boy?"

"I'm not very creative." I could feel my cheeks warm. "Although I did have an imaginary friend when I was a little girl. He was my best friend. We played hide-and-seek in my backyard." *Stop rambling. Why are you rambling?* I cleared my throat. "So can you help . . . you know, clean Boy up a little?"

"Normally, I don't have immediate availability, but my ten o'clock just canceled. I don't take walk-ins, but this looks like an emergency. Isn't that right, little one?" Boy wagged his filthy tail.

"How much to groom?" I asked, bracing myself.

"Well, for a dog this size and with this much work needed, it would run you about a hundred fifty."

"Dollars?" I asked, surprised. So much for eating for the next few days.

Sebastian laughed. "This one's on the house, though. It's the least I can do for a good Samaritan."

"You don't have to do that." I had become distrustful of favors. Favors often required payback. And having been married to Joe, I knew payback could be hurtful. Literally.

"I know I don't," Sebastian said. "But I want to."

I smiled and looked away. Those damn green eyes. They looked trustworthy. I was feeling an attraction, and that was the last thing I needed to feel. Joe's eyes had looked trustworthy, too, in the beginning.

"My next appointment is at eleven thirty," Sebastian said. "Come back around then, and Boy should be done."

"Thanks," I said, putting the dog into Sebastian's hands. When I did, I got a whiff of his cologne, which, unfortunately, was as alluring as his eyes.

"I'll be back soon," I told Boy, giving his little dirty head a kiss.

"Don't worry. I'll take good care of him. Here . . ." He pushed a notepad toward me. "Leave your number. This way, if there are any problems or if I finish earlier, I can call you. And your name again was . . ."

Clever, Mr. Green-Eyed Groomer. I never said. I toyed with the idea of giving a different name, but it would have been too much to keep track of. "Clara."

"Clara. Good. I was beginning to think it was a secret." He smiled, his green eyes crinkling.

I wrote down the number of the burner phone and started walking backward toward the exit as Sebastian took Boy into the back. I had the urge to ask if I could stick around and watch, and I wasn't sure if it was because I didn't want to leave the dog or because I didn't want to leave Sebastian.

"Oh, one more thing," Sebastian said, suddenly popping his head back out. "Um, this is a little awkward . . ."

"That's fine," I said. "Awkward is my middle name." Oh no, wait . . . was he going to ask me out on a date? I couldn't say yes, of course. But what reason would I give?

"Well, Clara, you see . . ." He looked like he was searching for the right words.

"I'm sorry, um, Sebastian," I stuttered, "I don't think—"

"Your wig is on backward," he said finally.

If I thought my cheeks had warmed before, they were officially on fire now. I touched the side of my head. "My wig?"

"Just thought you should know in case you wanted to fix it before you leave. There's a mirror over there." He pointed to a social media wall that resembled a Hollywood red carpet. "Personally, I think it looks nice on you either way," he added before slipping back behind the swinging door and disappearing.

Chapter 12

AFTER QUICKLY ADJUSTING MY wig, I couldn't get out of there fast enough. Well, that was embarrassing. But who cares? I wasn't there to make a good impression. This wasn't a date. I was there to get my dog . . . I mean, *the* dog groomed and presentable before finding him a home. Now, what was I going to do for an hour and a half?

More tourists were milling around, a few of them dressed like witches with black-and-white striped leggings. Maybe I could play tourist for a while before I had to leave Salem for good. Things were getting too complicated. Neighbors. Dogs. Green-eyed groomers. I needed to find a safe place for Boy and then plan my next safe house.

"I thought you'd never come out of there."

Beckett was standing next to me, looking annoyed.

"What are you doing here?" I whispered, putting my hand in front of my face like a football coach calling plays to a quarterback.

"What do you think? Waiting for you. We need to start the investigation."

"I told you. I'm not a professional detective."

"We made a deal."

"Yes, I know. And I'll hold up my end. I know you think you were murdered—I know you truly believe that—but I just don't want you to get your hopes up with my sleuthing skills."

"I'll take my chances."

With Beckett at my side, I started walking down Essex Street, looking at each person I passed and checking to see if they noticed Beckett. None did. What was so special about me that I could see ghosts? And when, exactly, did I attain this superpower?

"So, what's the plan?" Beckett asked.

"Um . . ." I found myself distracted by the glory of Essex Street, which looked to be the hub of Salem, the place tourists flocked to in the fall. I could see why. The cobblestone street. The red brick facades. The quaint restaurants and shops. It didn't seem all that different from what it must have been during colonial times. I thought of those poor women and men branded as witches and whose deaths would ignite a tourism frenzy. Above, the sun was shining brightly. If I hadn't been on the run and tricked into finding a murderer, I would have loved to take a stroll, take in a museum, learn about the Salem Witch Trials. I scanned the storefronts, realizing I hadn't had anything to eat since I had given the rest of my beef jerky to Boy that morning. I walked toward a donut shop.

"Where are you going?" Beckett asked.

"I need to get something to eat."

"At a time like this?"

"Yes. I'm sure you remember humans require sustenance."

The line for a place called The Haunted Cookie was long and out the door, which I took as a good sign that there was some delicious goodness inside.

"We're wasting time," Beckett said, standing next to me.

"We don't have to be," I whispered. A couple in front of me turned around when I spoke, and I smiled at them. "Sorry." I reached into my pocket and held up my burner as if I was talking to someone.

"What do you mean?" Beckett asked as they turned back around.

I typed into my phone:

Tell me what happened while we wait.

"Good idea," Beckett said. "See? You *are* good at this. Okay, so . . ." He took a deep breath that was really no breath at all. "I got up yesterday morning at my usual time. Around six or so. Then I ate. When I'm home on break, my mom makes me pancakes with bananas and strawberries in the shape of a happy face. Then I went for a run . . ."

"A happy face, really?" I asked, holding the phone to my ear.

"She likes to, okay?"

The line was moving quickly, and before I knew it, I was at a large display case with trays of donuts of every color and cupcakes the size of a small dog. I thought about Boy and hoped he was all right.

"Are you listening to me?" Beckett asked.

"Mmmm hmmm," I said, my mouth watering. I had my eye on a donut billed as a Fluffernutter, filled with peanut butter cream and topped with vanilla frosting, chocolate chips, and some kind of peanut butter crumble. Joe had been allergic to peanut butter, so we were never allowed to have any in the house. I couldn't count how many times I thought about dropping a clump of it into his mouth while he was sleeping. But as much as I was hurting, I wasn't a killer. I was determined to be better than him. So peanut butter was just one of the many things I had to do without while being married to Joe.

"Can I help you?" asked a young woman with large-rimmed glasses and a checkered apron. Her nametag read *Alice*.

"I'll have the Fluffernutter, please," I said, tempted to ask for a chocolate banana cupcake, too, but I refrained. I was already pushing it with the Fluffernutter. My body might go into shock after the entire package of cookies I had eaten the night before, following my beef jerky and rotisserie chicken feast.

"I seriously think you're not listening to a word I say," Beckett said.

"I'm concentrating at the moment."

"Yeah, I can see that." Beckett seemed antsy. "It's weird being here," he said as Alice deftly maneuvered around two other workers handling orders.

"Why? Did you come here often?"

"Not in a while, but yes. Alice and I dated for a while. Her mom owns the place."

"Really?" I said, a bit too loud, catching Alice's attention.

"Sorry," I said, pointing to my phone again.

"Why are you so surprised?" he asked.

Alice didn't seem like Beckett's type. Not that I really knew his type, but Maggie, the girl he had been arguing with at Derby's, seemed more outgoing, forward, and loud, judging by the way she handled herself. She was someone not afraid to make a scene and let everyone around her know how displeased she was. Alice seemed more reserved.

Alice pulled a piece of bakery paper from a box and stuck her hand into the display. She plopped the Fluffernutter into a paper bag. "Anything else?" she asked in a tiny voice.

"No, I think that's it," I said. If Alice really had dated Beckett, I was sure she must have heard the news about the accident. She didn't seem too broken up about it. But I knew that didn't really mean anything. Any one of the people I had spoken with over the past eight years had no idea how miserable I was on the inside.

Alice went to the register and punched a few buttons. "That's four seventy-nine."

I handed her a five-dollar bill and smiled at her when she gave me my change. "Thanks."

"Have a nice day," she said without even a glance at Beckett, who was staring at her, and moved onto the next customer.

Not far from The Haunted Cookie was an empty bench. I sat on it, taking out my donut.

"You know how many calories are in that thing?" Beckett asked, standing in front of me.

"Yes, and I don't care." For my entire marriage, I'd had Joe looking over my shoulder, commenting on everything I put in my mouth. Now, a ghost was doing the same? Just my luck. Why couldn't a ghost with a sweet tooth have found me instead?

"Are you ready to hear the rest of my story now?" Beckett asked.

"Yes," I said with a mouthful of Flutternutter. "Go ahead."

"Okay, so, like I was saying, me and Maggie didn't really end on good terms."

"You said that?" I asked.

Beckett gave an exasperated sigh. "You really *weren't* listening to a word I said in there." He pointed to The Haunted Cookie.

"Sorry. You have my full attention now, though." I took another big bite of my donut.

"Okay, Maggie and I started dating after Alice and I broke up."

"Why did you break up with Alice?"

"It's a long story, but basically we had grown apart."

"How long had you dated?"

"About three years."

"That's a long time to date someone."

"I guess, but I was away at school, and she was here, so we barely saw each other. And then one day, Maggie and I were hanging out, and you know, things happen."

"While you were still dating Alice?" *I think I just found my first murder suspect.*

"Anyway, Alice found out, and her mom essentially banned me from The Haunted Cookie."

"Do you think Alice could have something to do with your murder?"

"I don't know. She did have a bit of an anger management problem."

"Alice did?" I thought about the girl who had waited on me politely.

"Very passive-aggressive. Yeah, I find that shy girls often are. Either they're meek and quiet or they want to rip your head off."

Had Beckett given Alice a reason to rip his head off? Yes, he had cheated on her.

"And she *was* at Derby's yesterday," Beckett said.

"She was?" I tried to think of all the people I had seen and suddenly remembered her! Alice had been the one lingering in the baking aisle, staring at the sprinkles. "I think I almost hit her with my shopping cart." I could see her clearly in my mind, standing there, like she was going out of her way not to make an impression. To blend in with her surroundings. Kind of like I was doing. Or *trying* to do. And failing miserably. "Go on with your day yesterday," I said, suddenly intrigued. I took another bite of my Flutternutter.

"After my run, I showered and decided to walk to Derby's. I thought I could talk to Maggie before it got crowded. It didn't work out the way I planned."

"You think? Why was she so mad?"

Shockingly, Beckett appeared to be at a loss for words. He pulled down on the drawstring of his Harvard hoodie. "We were dating and . . . you know . . . intimate. And I took some photos of her that . . . well, somehow got sent to everyone on my WhatsApp contacts list."

"Somehow?"

"I *didn't* do it. I don't know how it happened. Somebody must have taken my phone and sent them."

A likely story. I took another bite of my donut. "Are you sure you didn't send them?"

"No! I wouldn't do that. You know, unless I was mad at her or something."

"Lovely."

"I *didn't send them*," he said sternly. "You have to believe me."

The problem was, I did believe him. I had spent eight years learning the contours of a face when it lied. Beckett wasn't lying. Or at least he didn't think he was. But now another person besides Alice was upset with Beckett. His ex-girlfriend, Maggie. "Do you think Maggie could have something to do with your murder?"

"I don't know anymore." Beckett sat down next to me on the bench.

"Look, Beckett!"

"What?"

"You're sitting down and not falling through the bench! You're engaging with the physical world!"

Beckett looked down at his legs, but the moment he realized he was sitting, he fell through to the sidewalk. "Wait, what happened?"

"I don't know. Maybe the whole crossing realms thing has to do with unconscious acceptance in addition to intention."

"Say what now?" he asked, standing up.

"Well, you walk around on the ground because that's an accepted part of your every day. You probably don't even think about it. And you sat down, expecting the bench to hold you. But once you became self-conscious about it, something changed."

"Wow, maybe you're right. You're pretty good at this ghost thing, you know."

No, I didn't know. And I didn't want to be. "What happened after your argument with Maggie? You didn't leave the market."

"I went into the back to see some friends and also to see Devon to get my last check. He said he would mail it, but I never received it. I figured I was there, so I'd pick it up. I really wanted to see him, too. To apologize."

Apologize? "You worked at Derby's?"

"Yeah, for, like, four years."

"Did you quit?"

"No, he fired me."

"Why did he fire you?"

Beckett was quiet again. Good Lord, how many people had reason to kill this guy?

"Well, I was throwing parties in the backroom at Derby's after the store closed."

"Parties?"

"Just a few friends. Nothing major. I had been doing it for years, never got caught. Grabbing beer from the refrigerators and handing them out to whoever came by after work."

"So, you were stealing, too."

"I guess, *technically*."

"And you got caught?"

"Yeah, some of the kids who came by were underage, and somehow the cops showed up one day. Devon nearly got his business license suspended because of it. And the president of the local parent-teacher association was calling for a boycott of Derby's, too."

"Wow, for something he didn't even do."

"Whose side are you on?" Beckett asked.

"I'm on no one's side."

"Well, that's why I wanted to see Devon. I wanted to tell him I was sorry. It was a stupid thing to do."

"No kidding. What happened after that?"

"I couldn't find him at first, but then I did, and he essentially threw me out," Beckett said, looking sad. "I guess I can't blame him. Then, as I was walking home, I started feeling bad."

"Define *bad*."

"Odd, you know? Not like myself. I started feeling worse and worse. Kinda dizzy. My vision was kinda blurry. And I was a bit nauseated."

"Did you eat anything after your mom's pancakes?"

"Not much. Just a couple of donut samples on the way to Derby's."

"Donut samples?"

"Yeah, from The Haunted Cookie."

"I thought you said you were banned from there."

"Early in the morning, there are usually samples outside. I grabbed a few."

"Nice loophole." Had Alice seen him coming and poisoned the samples? That seemed risky. An unsuspecting tourist might take one by mistake.

"And then I had some chocolate pastries that were outside Haute Chocolate. Sissy puts samples out early, too, to entice people to come inside. They're *soooo* good."

"So, let me get this straight . . . you had happy-face pancakes, donut samples, and chocolate pastries? Anything else?"

Beckett thought for a moment. "Oh, yeah, Devon had just put out a tray of cubed ham and cheese to sample. I took a few of those before I spoke to him."

"Devon? The guy who nearly lost his business license because of you?"

Beckett's brows furrowed. "Are you saying Devon tried to poison me?"

"I don't know. He certainly had a motive. To be honest, I'm surprised you didn't die from high cholesterol the way you eat."

"Funny."

"Did you eat anything after you left Derby's?"

"No, I think that's it. I was walking home, and that's when I started feeling weird. I knew something wasn't right, and I just wanted to get home."

"Like a medical emergency?"

"Yeah. Kinda."

"Why didn't you call 911 or something?"

"My house isn't too far from yours. I thought I could tough it out and get home, ask my mom what she thought. But I don't know what happened after that. I don't even remember walking into the street in front of Mrs. Birchgirdle."

I watched Beckett carefully. He seemed to be telling the truth. Officer Callahan mentioned an eyewitness for the accident. Maybe that person could corroborate his story.

"I had never felt that sick in my life," Beckett said. "It felt *wrong*. That's the only way I can explain it. I was fine and then I wasn't." He tried kicking a pebble that was on the sidewalk, but his foot went right through it. "This really sucks. I miss kicking stuff. I miss my life."

"I know you do." I wanted to console him but wasn't sure I could. A woman and a shaggy-looking dog were passing us, and the dog began barking forcefully at Beckett.

"I'm so sorry," the woman said, puzzled and pulling hard on her dog's leash. "He never does this. He's usually very friendly." When her dog wouldn't let up, she looked at me suspiciously, as dog owners are prone to do when their dogs seem to dislike someone.

I smiled at the woman as if there was absolutely, positively, no ghost standing next to me, and she finally managed to pull her dog away. When I turned around to resume my conversation with Beckett, he was gone.

Chapter 13

The little bell rang as I opened the door to The Pampered Pup. I could see Sebastian in the back, clipping the nails of a large dog. He waved to me. There were three dogs behind him, two that looked like goldendoodles badly in need of a haircut and one cute little thing that was jumping up on its hind legs, a black bowtie clipped to the top of its head. But there was no sign of Boy. My pulse quickened.

"Where's my dog?" I asked accusingly as soon as Sebastian stepped through the swinging door. Did I just say *my*?

"Easy there, John Wick," Sebastian said with a laugh, pointing to the back. "He's right there."

"Right where?"

Sebastian walked through the swinging door and picked up that little cute dog with the bowtie. He carried him to me and was about to place him in my arms, but the dog decided to jump into my arms instead.

"This is my dog?" I asked, trying to hold on to his wiggly body.

"I know, right? What a difference. He feels so much better, don't cha, Boy?"

Boy was busy licking my face. I couldn't remember any time somebody was so happy to see me. Except maybe my dad. "Aren't you a handsome boy?" I said, planting a kiss on Boy's wet nose.

"I think he's a Shih Tzu. If I had to guess, about three or four years old. For his hair to grow so long and be so matted, he would have had to be on his own for a while. The bad news is . . . he doesn't have a microchip."

"How do you know?"

"I have a scanner here." Sebastian pointed toward the back. "A long time ago, when I opened, I . . . um . . ." He seemed embarrassed. "I gave the wrong dog back to the wrong owner. Two dogs came in that looked identical. I vowed I would never make that mistake again. Live and learn, right? So, what are you going to do?"

"I don't know. I can't have a dog. I just . . . can't."

"It's a shame because you two look pretty great together." He smiled. "The Salem Animal Shelter is only a couple of blocks from here. You can try there, see if anyone is looking for a lost dog. Ask for Bentley. He's a good guy. Tell him I sent you." Sebastian walked behind the counter, reached into a bucket, and handed me a red leash. "This really isn't a proper leash, but at least you have something, so you don't have to hold him the whole way. He'll probably have to pee."

"Okay, but let me pay for the leash. You've been so nice, and I really wish you'd let me pay you for the grooming."

"Like I said, good Samaritans should be rewarded. Professional courtesy. The leash is on the house, too. And, seriously, no strings."

Strings. I found myself wanting them this time. Those green eyes. They seemed honest and kind. I looked for signs of duplicity—lack of eye contact, a muscle twitch—but there was none. "Thank you." I picked up Boy's neatly trimmed paw and waved it. "Boy thanks you, too."

"Anytime," Sebastian said. "Well, I'd better get back to work. These dogs don't groom themselves."

I walked outside, resisting the urge to look behind me. What was I doing? I couldn't be flirting with a dog groomer. I didn't care how green his eyes were. I placed Boy on the ground, and he immediately walked with his clean, shaved little legs toward the curb and peed.

"Yay! I'm so proud of you!" I said as if my child had just graduated from high school. "Okay, let's go see if anyone's been looking for you."

The Salem Animal Shelter was . . . well, a zoo. Dozens of cages filled with barking dogs. The place looked neat and clean, and the cages looked spacious, but it was clearly overrun with animals. They looked well cared for, but very, very lonely.

A middle-aged man was behind a barricade, putting one of the dogs back into a cage after petting its furry head. He looked up at me as I approached. "Hi, what can I do for you?"

"Hi, are you Bentley?" I looked for a name tag, but he had none.

"Yes, that's me."

"Hi, Sebastian, over at The Pampered Pup, suggested I stop by and talk to you."

"Well, you found me!" he said loudly so that I could hear him over the din of the dogs. I found myself shouting, too.

"I was wondering if there was anyone who had reported a missing dog!"

Bentley shook his head and glanced at Boy. "No, afraid not. Why, is that dog lost?"

Instinctively, my hands tightened around Boy. "No, this is my dog." *What am I doing?* "I was asking . . . for a friend. She found one in her yard."

Bentley shook his head. "That's terrible. What does the dog look like?"

"Look like?" I petted Boy's head. "Well, he's, um . . ."

"It's a boy?"

"Yes, a boy. He kind of looks like mine." I brought Boy up to my face, and he began licking my cheeks.

"Looks like yours, huh," Bentley said, skeptical, eyeing the temporary leash that Sebastian had given me. "Well, no one, as far as I know, has reported a missing dog. But if you would like to leave your number, I can contact you if someone comes looking."

"That would be great." I gave Bentley the number for my burner phone that I was giving to way too many people.

"You can check the library and town hall, too. There are bulletin boards there. Maybe there's a lost dog notice," Bentley suggested. "And you can tell your . . . friend that, if they want, they can make up their own sign and place it there. Maybe someone will see it. I'd be happy to hold on to the dog in the meantime, if they can't."

"That's very nice of you," I said, although I had a feeling the dogs in the shelter might eat Boy for lunch. "I'll . . . um, I'll let her know. Thank you, Bentley."

I walked quickly out of the shelter and took a deep, cleansing breath. Seeing those dogs in cages had triggered me. No one, human or pet, belonged in a cage—a literal one or figurative one. I looked at Boy in my hands, his little eyes peering up at me.

"All right, all right," I said. "You win. Let's go home."

Chapter 14

After a quick stop at a place called Bow-wow Bones & Biscuits to buy a proper leash, harness, collar, a pet carrier, and enough dog food to feed this little guy for a year, Boy and I headed home. What I *should* have been doing was buying Sharpies and paper so I could make *Lost Dog* signs to post at the library and town hall, like Bentley suggested.

What is wrong with me?

I was trying not to panic. Why did I buy a pet carrier? It seemed logical at the time. At least, the middle-aged woman, Gladys, who owned Bow-wow Bones & Biscuits, seemed to think so and somehow convinced me my "precious little dear" deserved the highest-quality dog food, too. She must have seen dollar signs on my forehead when I walked in.

"Someone's attached," Beckett said, appearing next to me and motioning toward Boy.

"Hi! Where have you been? I was worried about you." Boy looked up at Beckett but didn't bark. He hadn't barked at William, either. Maybe he had seen his fair share of ghosts while he was surviving out there in the cruel Salem undergrowth. He seemed like a smart dog. He already knew the way home.

"Yeah, right. You were worried about me?" Beckett asked.

"No, seriously. You just disappeared."

"I thought that's what you wanted."

So did I. I was learning a lot of new things about myself this week.

"It's just . . ." Beckett fake-breathed in. "It's like I said. I miss my life. It was taken away from me."

I suddenly felt guilty for thinking about myself. Things could always be worse. I knew that. Even when I was living with Joe, I tried to focus on the big picture. I always told myself that I could be dead or really sick and that as long as I was alive, there was hope. Poor Beckett couldn't say that. "Don't worry. I already have some ideas about who to talk to."

"You do?" Beckett asked, brightening.

"Yeah, I was thinking it might be a good idea to talk to the eyewitness to the accident. But . . ."

"But what?"

"Finding out who that is means I might have to go to Officer Callahan. And I'd rather not have to talk to anyone in law enforcement."

"Why not?"

"Long story."

"Yeah, well, you don't have to anyway," Beckett said. "I know who the eyewitness is."

"You do?"

"I tried to talk with her after Mrs. Birchgirdle hit me with her car, but she didn't see me. She was focused on my body. You know, my *body*."

"Who was it?"

"Stephanie Hastings. She runs one of the touring companies here. It's not far from The Haunted Cookie."

That didn't surprise me. Nothing seemed terribly far in downtown Salem. "Do you know which touring company?"

"I don't really remember, but it shouldn't be hard to find," Beckett said. "There's a great big pumpkin—a fake one—right outside her storefront. It's popular for selfies."

"That's great. I'll head over there and see if I can find out anything."

Beckett's mood seemed better as we arrived at my house. We had made some progress, and people—human or, apparently, ghost—appreciated when their concerns were taken seriously.

We walked into the driveway, and I put my bags down to find my key. Boy was waiting patiently at my feet. As soon as the door opened, Boy went running in like he had been living there for years. I dropped the leash and let him go, stepping inside.

"I'll let you know what I find out," I said to Beckett. "Or, better yet, you can go with me, if you'd like, to see Stephanie. Maybe something will come to you while I meet with her."

He stood there looking at me.

"What's the matter?" I asked.

"Are you seriously still not inviting me in?" he asked.

"Um . . ." I knew it was rude, and I didn't expect Beckett to understand, but I needed my space. And I had a feeling Beckett wouldn't be amenable to the same deal I had made with William—knock or holler first, enter second. "I just need some time to myself. I'll head out again this afternoon for some more snooping." And to get more food, of course. *There goes another two hundred dollars.* "I promise I'll make some headway."

Beckett looked unconvinced, but he disappeared, and I closed the door. Boy was sitting in the entryway dutifully, and I took off his new leash and harness. He immediately went to the makeshift water bowl and took a drink. I had mistakenly told Gladys at the pet store that I fashioned food and water bowls for Boy out of the home's old china, and she gladly let me know those might contain lead. Next thing I knew, I had overpriced water and food bowls in my cart.

I put the pet carrier on the table and began taking the dog's things out of the shopping bags. I thought about putting the food in the cabinets, but there was no need to make myself at home. I needed to be ready to split at a moment's notice. I washed the new dog bowls and filled them with food and water, and as I was placing them near the front door, I heard a noise in the kitchen. I looked, but there was nothing there.

My mind went immediately to Joe, and my knees buckled. I surveyed the array of items on the dining table. It looked like I was manning a table at a flea market, but there was nothing I could use for a weapon. I glanced at the pet carrier, wondering whether I should return it, when I heard the noise again. I would have thought I was hearing things, but even Boy lifted his head from the dog bowl and peered into the kitchen.

I took a step forward. "William, is that you? I thought we had a deal."

Silence.

"William?"

"Yes?"

A book floated toward me from the library, and then William appeared, holding it. "Did you summon me?"

"I thought we were going to respect each other's privacy."

"Indeed."

"Were you in the kitchen?"

William held up the book. "I was reading in the adjacent chamber."

Another noise from the kitchen. This time, I could detect its location. It came from somewhere under the sink. A rat? Was Joe hiding under there? Impossible. He wouldn't fit. I took a few more steps, bent down, and peered at the cabinetry. "Did you hear—?"

Suddenly, *something* on four legs walked straight out of the closed kitchen cabinet and began strutting across the floor.

"What the . . ." I fell backward and hit my head on Boy's water bowl, soaking the back of my hair. "What is *that*?" I asked, pointing to the pale gray, four-legged thing taking a leisurely stroll into the dining room.

"'Tis a cat," William said nonchalantly.

"You're kidding me. A ghost cat? Where did it come from?"

"My grandson Joseph did bring him into the household one day, and . . . alas, the cat's tenure was brief. Joseph was not of a compassionate nature." William looked down, as if ashamed. "The cat has dwelt here with me ever since."

"Um, you could have mentioned that, you know."

I kept my eye on the animal, which resembled a Siamese cat and was looking right at me as if to say, *What are YOU doing here?* I stood up and shook the water out of the back of my hair. *I'm with you, Ghost Cat. What AM I doing here?*

Ghost Cat walked toward Boy, who got down on his front two legs in a playful stance and then went running around the dining table and into the library and back, stopping again in front of the cat, who looked at him curiously.

"So, the cat lives here?" I asked.

"For the most part. I have glimpsed her in the yard on occasion."

"It's a girl?"

"I reckon so."

Ghost Cat appeared uninterested in the dog and walked through a wall under the stairs. *Nice going*, I said to myself. Now I had a human ghost, a ghost cat, and a real dog living with me, and another human ghost hovering around outside who wanted something from me. *What happened to no attachments?*

"You seem preoccupied," William said.

Talk about an understatement. "Never mind. I have to step out to get more food and . . ." I didn't want to get into Beckett's dilemma. "I also have some money issues, but that's my problem."

"Might I be of aid in any manner?" William asked.

"No, that's very sweet of you, and I'm sorry. I didn't mean to be snippy. This isn't your fault. I need to clean up my own mess." I wrapped my arms around myself. "It's chilly in here."

"Would you prefer I kindle another fire?"

"Better not until the sun goes down. I don't want to risk someone seeing the smoke." I bent down and patted Boy on his newly groomed head and straightened his little bowtie. "I'll be back in a little while." I reached for one of the over-priced dog toys I had been duped into buying and threw it toward the library room. Boy chased after it eagerly. Maybe now he would leave my wig alone.

I took another two hundred dollars and checked my money situation. I was down to just over three hundred. That wasn't going to get me far. With the way things were going, I would have to ask Bentley at the Salem Animal Shelter if there was room for two.

Chapter 15

BECKETT WAS RIGHT. IT was easy to find Stephanie's Triple H Touring Company, which was located across the street from The Haunted Cookie. Three young women dressed as the Sanderson Sisters from *Hocus Pocus* were posing next to an enormous pumpkin outside, and there were a few tables and chairs occupied by people reading brochures. Inside, a woman was standing behind a counter.

"Beckett, are you here?" I whispered, stepping away from the storefront. He hadn't been near the house. Where did ghosts go? I pulled out my burner, pretended to make a call, and put the phone to my ear. "Hey, Beckett. I'm here. Are you coming?" I waited. "Beckett?!" I said louder, as if we had a bad connection. I scanned the area and didn't see him anywhere.

Looks like I'm on my own. I opened the door and walked inside.

The woman at the counter had a bob haircut and a jacket that looked as if Jackson Pollack used it as a practice canvas. I couldn't remember the last time I had seen that much color on one garment. She was looking at a computer screen and typing on a keyboard. When she saw me coming, she smiled broadly. "Are you here for the two p.m. tour?"

"Um, no," I said, looking around at the posters on the walls.

"There's plenty of room since it's the offseason," she said. "Right around September and October, though, we're bound to book up." She leaned down as if to tell me a secret. "You didn't hear this from me, but the prices go up in the fall, too." She stuck out her hand. "I'm Stephanie. I'm the owner."

"Nice to meet you." I shook her hand, impressed. She looked to be in her early thirties, like me, and was already running her own business. I often wondered what I would have become if I hadn't married Joe. "Actually, I'm not here for a tour."

"Oh?" Her brows furrowed.

I wanted to ask about Beckett's accident but stopped myself. Maybe the direct route wasn't the way to go about things. People didn't like to be interrogated. I picked up a brochure from the counter. "I mean, I'm not here for a tour *today*. I am thinking about later in the week."

"Oh, that's absolutely fine," Stephanie said with a smile. "You can book it online, if you'd like, or I'd be happy to do it for you here." She punched a few keys. "What kind of tour are you interested in? We do History, Hauntings, and *Hocus Pocus*. Hence, the Triple H."

"History, I guess." I had had enough of hauntings.

"What day were you thinking of?"

"Hmmm . . ." I pretended to think. "I was planning on coming yesterday, but then there was that terrible accident on my corner and . . ."

Stephanie stopped typing. "Oh, my. You know, I saw that."

"You *did*?" I asked as if I didn't already know.

She lowered her voice so that two young men on the other side of the room didn't hear. "It was terrible."

"I saw an old woman."

"That was Mrs. Birchgirdle. Poor thing. She tried her best, she really did, but I don't know what had gotten into Beckett Miller. Mrs. Birchgirdle had her hand pressed on her horn. I happened to be on my way to work, and I saw her coming, but before I could call out to Beckett, he was hit. Just terrible."

"He just didn't see her?" I asked, my voice raising up weirdly in my attempt to sound shocked.

"He was . . . I can't explain it. Acting strangely. Like he couldn't see well. It's possible he was listening to some music—I saw earbuds in his ears—but it seemed like more than that. As I told Officer Callahan, he was doing this weird jerky movement. So strange. I wish I could have helped him. I feel so guilty."

I could relate. I was feeling pretty guilty myself at this point, lying about my reason for being here. "Well," I held up a brochure. "I'll book the tour on my own when I figure out my schedule. It was so nice to meet you."

"Same here," Stephanie said. "Enjoy your time in Salem!"

Outside, I headed toward Derby's Downtown Market, tossing around the new information I had learned from Stephanie in my mind. Her description of Beckett acting strangely synced with what Beckett had been describing about the way he felt. Like some kind of medical emergency. Maybe he *had* been poisoned. But by whom?

I took out my phone. "Beckett!" I said into the receiver. "Beckett, are you there?!"

Where could this kid be?

As I approached Derby's, I saw the chocolate store that Beckett had mentioned. Haute Chocolate. A tiny storefront on the other side of the street, which was probably why I had missed it before.

I crossed at the intersection and walked toward the array of chocolate samples displayed on a circular table draped with a white tablecloth. My mouth watered. Dark chocolate. Milk chocolate. Chocolate with caramel. With cherries. No wonder Beckett had plopped some into his mouth. They were irresistible. I was about to reach for one when I remembered why I was here. If Beckett had been poisoned, it was very possible the poison had come from one of these delectable-looking desserts. Talk about death by chocolate!

"Can I help you?" A sixty-something woman with long, curly gray hair in a stylish pantsuit walked toward me from the store entrance. "I'm Sissy."

"Hi, Sissy. I'm Clara." *Why did you say that? Stop introducing yourself!* "I was just about to go food shopping but was lured here by your lovely treats."

"Well, that's the idea." She smiled. "Glad it's working. Can I interest you in some chocolate? We have a lot more in the store."

"Sure," I said, wondering how I could turn the conversation to Beckett, but then she gave me an easy entry.

"When did you arrive in Salem?" she asked, stepping behind a counter full of chocolate in every color and shape.

"Right around the time of that horrible accident," I said and watched her closely, looking for signs of deception, but her face fell.

"How awful." She shook her head. "The Miller family have been customers of mine for years. A lovely family. I know some people have said things about Beckett over the years, and he was by no means a saint, but we all have our problems and our troubles, and I think people are very quick to judge. He was a good kid and far too young to be taken away. When you get to my age, you understand how very fragile and special life is."

Wow, either this woman was in no way responsible for Beckett's death or she deserved an Academy Award. My gut was telling me it was the former. "He sounds like a special young man," I said.

"We're all special, young lady. It's just that some of us haven't realized it yet."

Chapter 16

DERBY'S DOWNTOWN MARKET WAS more crowded than last time, probably because it was the afternoon. I grabbed a shopping cart, placing my goodie bag from Haute Chocolate in the child seat. The last thing I needed was luxury chocolate, but if I was going down financially, apparently, I was going down big!

I headed into the prepared foods section, grabbing the last rotisserie chicken (whew!), and then got in the deli line. At this point, I imagined I had so many nitrates in my system I could make money using my body as a lab experiment.

I glanced around the display cases to see which deli meats were on sale. How ironic that my dog was getting premium food while I was getting the stuff with the fillers and coloring agents. What was wrong with this picture?

"Can I help you?" asked a man behind the counter.

It was the guy I had seen yesterday watching Simon. Devon. His nametag confirmed it. The guy who owned this place and nearly lost it because of Beckett Miller. I thought about starting up a conversation with him, and somehow getting around to asking about Beckett, but the deli counter was busy. And unlike Stephanie and Sissy, he didn't seem like the chatty type.

"I'll have a quarter pound of the turkey that's on sale," I said instead. "And a quarter pound of Swiss, sliced thin." The thinner the slices, the more I could convince myself I was getting from a quarter pound.

Devon nodded and went about unwrapping the meats. His eyes kept looking past me, and I turned around and saw Simon was again at his little table, surrounded by people. Simon kept glancing up at Devon; he seemed just as preoccupied with him as he had been the day before.

"Would you like anything else?" Devon extended his arm over the counter to hand me the turkey and cheese.

Yes, I'll take everything you have. I'm starving. "No, that's it. Thank you."

I pulled the cart away and headed toward Simon's table. I was ashamed to say that I was already craving another cold brew. I reached past a young couple debating whether or not to try Black Aye.

"It's pretty good." I reached for two more containers. "I bought one yesterday and came back for more."

Simon didn't look too pleased with me. Maybe I had interrupted his sales pitch. I wanted to say, *Hey, you think you got problems? I'm hiding from an abusive husband and trying to find a ghost's killer.*

I quickly went through the store—making sure I followed the arrows on the floor this time—to get a few more things. Thankfully, there were no shopping cart collisions, although that girl Alice was back in the baking section. She looked pensive, like she was thinking really hard about something. Was she in Derby's every day? Didn't she have any hobbies? And if she owned a donut shop, wouldn't she get her ingredients wholesale? Why bother paying retail prices?

Hmmm . . . kinda suspicious. Which made me wonder if this had something to do with Beckett's death.

As I walked toward the registers, that girl, Maggie, was sitting on a bench by the customer service desk. She was talking on the phone and looked peeved. Like Alice, she didn't look much like a grieving ex-girlfriend. I pretended to eye up the gift cards and pulled my cart next to her just as she ended the call. She sighed loudly—and dramatically—and then said, "Ick." I was beginning to see the attraction between her and Beckett. Two drama queens.

"Everything all right?" I asked innocently. How ironic. I fled my marriage because I had spent eight years pretending as a way of *withholding* information, and here I was pretending as a way of *accessing* information. I kept reminding myself that I was doing it for a good cause this time.

"I'm fine." Maggie flipped her hair behind her shoulders. "But men suck."

"That, they do."

Maggie looked at me. "Do I know you?"

"I don't think so. Although maybe you saw me here yesterday. I was in line when you and . . . your friend were arguing."

"Oh, that." Maggie shook her head. "You know, Beckett—that friend you saw—was in an accident right after that. He died."

"Oh no!" *Be believable.* "I'm sorry to hear that. Was he your boyfriend?"

"*Ex*-boyfriend. We had gotten into a fight. He turned out to be a jerk. But, still, nobody deserves that."

I watched her closely. Did she mean that? Was she telling the truth? "You miss him?"

She shrugged. "I guess I do. It sucks because you don't know when you have a fight with someone that that will be the last time you see them, and then you have to spend the rest of your life feeling guilty because you spent your last moments with them mad and screaming at them. Does that make sense?"

"It makes total sense," I said.

"And now I have to go to the funeral and look his parents in the face. I always liked his parents, and they probably hate me."

"I'm sure they don't hate you."

She pulled up the shirt sleeve on her right arm. "Beckett bought me this beautiful bracelet for my birthday last year. I don't know why I'm wearing it today, but I felt like I should." She looked at her watch. "Well, I'd better get back to work. Nice talking to you."

She got up and walked away, and all I could think was Maggie didn't have anything to do with Beckett's death. She seemed genuinely sad, even for someone who was so mad at Beckett the day before. I knew I wouldn't be good at this. How many suspects did that leave? And who was to say that someone completely unknown to me hadn't killed Beckett? Or that Beckett hadn't had some kind of non-murderous medical emergency, despite his certainty that he was murdered?

I got in one of the register lines and realized it was Beverly's. I thought about moving to another line, but the others were even longer. I had spent only ten minutes with Beverly since arriving in Salem but already knew she was the town gossip. Even as she scanned the items of the person two orders in front of me, I could tell she was listening to every conversation around her. Although—now that I thought about it—Beverly might be a good one to mine about Beckett's murder. She might have seen a thing or two.

The couple in front of me, a man and woman about my age, were putting their snacks on the conveyor belt. Bags of organic potato chips and two Snickers bars. I wondered which of the two had the sweet tooth. Probably the guy. The woman looked as grumpy as Simon over by the shelf-stable cold brew.

"I'm sorry," the man said to the woman, his eyebrows pushing upward. "There was nothing available."

"I told you we should have gotten something in advance," the woman said with a heavy sigh.

"It's offseason in Salem, Cindy. I thought we'd have a pick of the litter. How was I supposed to know that there'd be some big tech conference in Boston yesterday and today, booking up all the hotel rooms?"

Tech conference?

"I just need a bed. How hard is that?" The woman crossed her arms. "I'd rather not sleep in the car again."

The man said something else, but I didn't hear what it was. I had already abandoned my cart and was running out of the market.

Chapter 17

I TORE OPEN THE front door to the house and ran inside as Boy came running toward me. *How could I be so stupid?*

"May I enter?" William's voice asked.

"I don't know if now's a good time, William, but go ahead." I quickly started tossing all my garbage—rotisserie chicken carcass, empty seltzer cans—into paper bags and rolled the tops of them. Then I started throwing my clothing into my backpack.

"What is transpiring?"

"I forgot," I said, breathless, picking up the dog's bowls. "There's a big technology conference in Boston this week. It's like an East Coast version of Silicon Valley." There was no way Joe was going to miss it. Even if he didn't know where I was. *Especially* if he didn't know where I was, because he wouldn't want anyone to think he wasn't on top of his wife.

Literally and figuratively. "He always stops at this house after the conference. It's like the one time of year he comes here."

"Does he?" William asked, as if trying to remember.

"Yeah, he doesn't want to. He can't wait to sell this place, but he likes to make sure it's still standing. Or so he says. He says he only stays for a few minutes. He makes me stay in the hotel room. I never cared because I would use the time to call my dad. I completely forgot about the conference! When my dad died, all I thought about was running."

William's face changed. "I believe I've seen him before. Your husband."

I stopped moving. "Really?"

William nodded, but he had a weird look on his face. I didn't have time to ask.

"Well, then I believe you've met your great-great-great-great-grandson," I said.

I ran around the rest of the floor and tried to restore the home to the way it was before I arrived, collecting Boy's toys and refolding the blankets and putting them back on the pile where I had found them. I crossed my fingers that Joe didn't notice the ashes in the fireplace. I was about to hurry outside to put my garbage bag into Mr. Wiggins's trash can when a car pulled into the driveway.

Jesus . . . I peeked through the window.

A BMW. Joe! My heart pounded.

"He's here," I said to William. "You need to leave."

"But—"

"William, *please.*"

"As you wish," he said, disappearing. I fixed the chairs and shoved the garbage and all the dog's stuff into a bottom cabinet at the back of the kitchen, hoping Joe wouldn't open it. Then I grabbed the rest of my stuff into my arms and tore up the stairs, hiding everything under the bed. I opened the bedroom closet, took the folded-up plastic I had put there, placed it back on the bed, and stood there, surveying the room.

"I think that's everything," I said aloud. I just had to find a place to hide while Joe briefly inspected the house. Maybe he wouldn't come upstairs, I thought hopefully.

Bark!

Oh no! Boy!

I hurried back down the stairs where the little guy was trying unsuccessfully to follow me up, but the stairs were too high for him. I quickly lifted him and got to the top of the stairway when I heard a key enter the lock on the front door. I stood near the frilly twin bed, shaking.

A voice. Joe's voice. He was talking to someone. *Please don't let it be Mr. Wiggins!*

Then another voice. A woman's.

I knew that voice.

Rhonda Hooper.

Joe's realtor.

I leaned over the open stairway so I could hear better.

"Well, here we are again," Joe said. "And the house is just as disgusting as last time."

"Disgusting, maybe, but this house is worth *millions*," Rhonda said. "You're sitting on a goldmine here."

"So you've been telling me all these years." A pause. "Something looks different, doesn't it?"

My heart threw itself against my rib cage.

"What do you mean?" Rhonda asked, her high-pitched voice reverberating through the house.

"Dammit, something got in here. Do you see those little footprints?"

I held tightly onto Boy, who was squirming in my arms, trying to see who the new people with the new smells were. I carefully began walking toward the bedroom, tiptoeing around the squeaky floorboards.

"Oh, God, and it smells like urine," Joe said.

"I think something peed over here," Rhonda said. "I'll get on that right away. There's a great cleaning woman I use in the Boston area. Worth every penny. I'll have her stop by in a day or two."

"Great. Dumping more money into this place."

"It happens, Joe. This is an old house."

Bark!

Oh no!

"Did you hear that?" Joe asked.

"Hear what?"

"It sounded like it came from upstairs," Joe said.

Panic flushed through me as I hurried into the bedroom. *Think, think . . .*

The closet was too narrow for me to hide in and would probably be the first place Joe looked. Under the bed was a no-go with the dog. I was screwed. There was nowhere to go.

But then a latch moved, and the narrow door in the wall next to the closet opened. *The secret rooms.* Without wasting time, I ran through and found William standing there. He shut the door behind me and slid the deadbolt.

I held onto my dog and leaned against the wall. All I could hear was my heart beating in my ears. I was in a narrow room that looked like it was supposed to be a kitchen, but there were no appliances or anything. Daylight was streaming in and onto William's pale face. To my left was another room, also empty, except for a dusty desk chair without a desk. Air was coming in from the crevices of a door somewhere behind me. I kept petting Boy over and over, praying he wouldn't bark again, but he was staring at William.

"Do they know I'm here?" I whispered.

William held up his hand and then disappeared.

Muffled voices came from the other room, Joe's and Rhonda's, but I couldn't make out what they were saying. Then the narrow door moved slightly, and my breath hitched. *Joe was trying to get in.*

"I don't see a doorknob," Joe said into the wall. "Do you have a key for this door?"

He was only a couple of feet from me, separated by some beams and planks of wood. Rhonda said something in response, but it was garbled.

"Whatever," Joe said. "I gotta get back. Let's get at it."

Then it got quiet. I was listening closely and nearly screamed when William appeared.

"Are they gone?" I whispered, petting Boy.

"Not exactly," William said, his pale face tinging red.

And then I heard it.

A banging sound. Repetitive. And getting louder.

No way.

I slowly slid to the floor. "Seriously?"

"Out of wedlock." William shook his head disapprovingly.

"You knew, didn't you?" I whispered. "You said you had seen Joe. He's done this here before."

William's eyes searched the floor.

How long had this been going on? From the beginning of my marriage? From before?

As I listened to the rhythmic banging, I realized I didn't feel betrayed. I felt . . . nothing. When it came to Joe, my heart was empty. Or maybe frozen solid.

I didn't know how long I sat there with the dog on my lap and William looking mortified, but eventually the noises stopped and there was movement in another part of the house.

"They're leaving?" I asked William.

William disappeared, and I waited for what seemed like an eternity. When he came back, he said, "They've left the house."

I unlatched the narrow door and slowly opened it, expecting the dusty linens on the bed to be on the floor. But the bed had been made, as if nothing had happened.

"He's in his carriage . . . er, vehicle," William said as a car started.

With Boy in my arms, I tiptoed out of the bedroom, past the frilly twin bed and bathroom, and hurried down the stairs, making sure the front deadbolt was reengaged. Then I carefully peeked out the smudgy window. Joe and Rhonda were sitting in the front seat of Joe's BMW.

He's leaving. He's leaving.

Just as the car changed gears, Mr. Wiggins's front door opened, and the old man came hobbling out.

"Hello, hello!" He was waving at Joe.

Oh no. Please go back inside, Mr. Wiggins. Please.

The car changed gears again, and to my horror, Joe stepped out of the car with one foot. "Yes?" he said to Wiggins.

"Just wanted to say my hellos!"

Now Rhonda was out of the car, too, with her after-sex hair.

"And who do we have here?" Mr. Wiggins asked politely.

"I'm Joe Turner, and this is my realtor, Rhonda."

"Pleasure to meet you both," Wiggins said. "I wanted to tell you that I've met the lovely Clara! She reminds me so much of my Alma."

Joe stared at him. "I'm sorry, who?" he asked.

"Why, Clara, of course! My Alma was a beautiful blond as well. You're a lucky man!"

Joe and Rhonda exchanged glances. Rhonda raised her eyebrows.

"Yeah, well, good luck to you," Joe said as he and Rhonda got back into the car. He put the car into reverse and drove out of the driveway. Mr. Wiggins waved at them kindly before returning to his house and shutting the door.

I turned back toward the house. William was in front of me, perplexed. "Why was your husband not more inquisitive regarding your presence here? Our neighbor made mention of you by name."

I pulled out one of the dining chairs and sat down with Boy in my hands.

"Because," I said. "My name isn't really Clara."

Chapter 18

"Not Clara?" William asked, confused.

I shrugged my shoulders and placed Boy on the floor. I retrieved one of the dog's toys I had hidden, a brown woolly mammoth, and tossed it to him; he ran to it eagerly. "No. I wanted to start my life again. And when I got here and met you, I just . . . gave myself a new name. You're the first person—I mean . . . well, yes, *person*, I told it to. I've always loved that name. It was the name of someone I used to know."

"What is your real name?"

"Emily."

My stomach twisted. The word seemed strange on my tongue. For nearly a decade, my name had been uttered in Joe's deep and disturbing voice, and despite its connection to my parents, it was like my body had turned against it. "Emily

Becker. Then my name was Emily Turner, I guess, once I was married, although *Turner* never seemed to fit." I thought back to the day I had first laid eyes on Joe at the hotel, and the words began to tumble out. "Joe really knew what he was doing all along. He chose me carefully. I was working at my first job out of college. At a hotel in New York City. Not a four-star hotel. Not even a three-star, if I'm being honest, but I didn't care. I was excited. I was on my way, you know?" I looked up at William, who probably didn't know what I was talking about, but he was listening intently. "I majored in hospitality and tourism management, imagining myself traveling the world. Running a boutique hotel somewhere exotic. Somewhere a long way from here. My mistake was in thinking Joe would help me get there. That he would go with me. That I was part of a team." I wiped a tear from the corner of my eye. "He was so kind in the beginning. I thought he had seen something special in me. I was so young. But what he saw, though, was a woman with no attachments, other than a father she loved dearly—a father he could use against her. As leverage. He saw someone shy, who didn't have a lot of friends, so there would be no real allies looking out for me. Ironically, for eight years, I had been surrounded by many people—*Joe's* friends, *Joe's* colleagues—at parties, on vacation, and yet they never seemed to suspect." I looked at William. "People see what they want to see, I guess."

"Women have often been expected to fit into certain box-es."

"Yes, they have." I looked into William's blue eyes, filled with understanding.

"I knew in my own time that it wasn't right," he said. "My wife was denied the liberty to harbor aspirations, to have dreams."

I wanted to ask William about his wife, Flora. To ask why he thought he was here, haunting this chilly old house, instead of being with her. I wanted to ask what had happened to him, the nature of his death. He had died so young, even by late 1800s standards. But I didn't want to pry. People showed themselves in their own time. When they were ready. When they felt . . . safe.

"What course of action do you intend to pursue now?" he asked.

"It sounds like they're hiring a cleaning woman. I only have a day or two that I can stay. I'll have to come up with something."

"Might I be of assistance in any manner?"

"No, I don't think you can. But you've helped so much already."

William nodded. "Well, perhaps I will return to my book."

"What are you reading?"

"*The Great Gatsby.*"

"It's a classic. Are you enjoying it?"

"I've read it many times before. I've read every book in this house many times. Of all the books in the library, it's not my favorite, but some passages . . . stir my soul." He cleared his throat. "My favorite passage: 'All I kept thinking about, over and over, was, you can't live forever; you can't live forever.'" He let the quote hang in the air as he began to fade.

"William, thank you for your help," I said before he was gone. "You've been very kind to me."

"'Tis my pleasure," he said and vanished.

I glanced at Boy, who looked like he had already succeeded in ripping the tag off the expensive dog toy I bought for him. "I've gotta figure out what I'm doing. And fast, little one. I can't stay here much longer. Rhonda and her people will be back."

He looked up at me. *Bark!*

"Yeah, I know. I'm hungry, too. You first, and then me."

DERBY'S DOWNTOWN MARKET WAS closing in fifteen minutes when I walked in and hurried to the registers. I had been hoping my cart full of items would still be there, but it wasn't. I wondered what my odds were of getting a rotisserie chicken at this hour.

"Hey, weren't you the one who abandoned her cart?!" Beverly yelled. She spritzed some Windex on her conveyor belt.

"Yeah, that was me."

After a loud *tsk*, Beverly yelled, "Devon, she's back!"

The door to the store office opened, and Devon stuck out his head. After spying me, he closed the door, and when he opened it again, he was holding my rotisserie chicken, cold cuts, and bag of chocolate in his hands. He placed them into a shopping cart that I realized had been mine and began pushing it toward me.

"I kept the cart by the office, just in case," he said. "I put the perishables in the refrigerator so they wouldn't go bad."

"Wow, that was really nice of you. Thank you."

"No problem," Devon said. He nodded at Beverly and strode back toward the office as I began putting my items on the register's still-wet conveyor belt.

"So, what was the big emergency?" Beverly asked as she began scanning them.

Yeah, wouldn't *she* like to know? I'm sure my life would provide enough fodder for Beverly's gossip train for the next few months, at least. "I just forgot I left one of the stove burners on."

"*Hmpf*, stove burner, you say? You could have burned your bed-and-breakfast down. I'm assuming you're staying at a bed-and-breakfast and not a hotel, since you have a stove." Beverly smiled at her own perception. "Which one you staying at?"

"I thought that was on sale," I said, pointing to the cold brew and trying to change the subject.

"Since yesterday? Don't think so." She kept scanning, and before she could ask me another question, Maggie appeared. "Have a good night, Beverly!"

"You, too, my dear." Then she looked at me and leaned down as if about to speak in confidence. "That poor girl. The things she's had to endure. I was no fan of Beckett Miller, and far be it from me to want to see anyone end up six feet under, but that boy didn't have his head on straight."

I reached for a reusable bag and began packing my items, hoping that Beverly would continue talking. She did.

"And they'll probably take away old Mrs. Birchgirdle's driver's license for this. That woman is a killing machine on wheels. Selena's been imploring her mother to give up that ghost."

I had a ghost of my own I was hoping to give up, but I had made a promise to Beckett, and I wanted to try to keep it, even if I had to leave Salem quicker than expected. "I heard the accident."

"You heard about that?"

"No, I *heard* it."

Beverly stopped scanning. "What were you doing over there so early in the morning? Ain't no bed-and-breakfasts I can think of over there."

Boy, Beverly's mind was a processing machine. She was wasting her time at Derby's. She should have worked for the FBI. "I just happened to be outside."

"What did you see?"

I certainly had her interest, but I was here for *in*tel, not *to* tell. "Nothing, really. I just called the cops."

"Ah, so *you're* the one who called the cops. You're Clara?"

I tried not to appear startled, but I'm sure I was unsuccessful. News traveled fast. Officer Callahan was right. Salem was definitely a small town. "Yeah. That's me."

"Well, you did a good deed, Clara."

Before Beverly totaled up my order, I plucked a magazine from a nearby display. "I'll take this, too."

Beverly took the magazine and studied it, pulling it away from her face for her middle-aged eyes to read the cover. "You into history?"

"I've discovered an interest in it lately, yes."

Beverly scanned it. "I'm also going to have to charge you for two reusable bags. They're a dollar each."

Why not. If I'm going to the poorhouse, I'm going to need bags to hold my things. "That's fine. How much do I owe you?"

She gave me my total. I paid and slipped the magazine into one of my bags.

"Don't forget to bring your own bags next time. You get a nickel credit each time you use them." She handed me my receipt. "Glad you didn't burn down your bed-and-breakfast and that you were able to come back for your things. Have a nice night now, hon."

"You, too."

I left Derby's with my two shopping bags, and as I turned toward home, Beckett appeared, startling me.

"Did you find anything out?" he asked.

"Geez, you gotta quit sneaking up on me like that."

"I don't think I have a choice." He shrugged his shoulders.

"Well, I spoke to Stephanie at the touring company earlier today. She said you were acting strangely right before the accident."

"I told you. I wasn't myself. I felt terrible."

"Could you have had a stomachache from breakfast?"

"You *clearly* have never had my mom's pancakes. They are *to die for*—I mean that in a good way. But . . . I was thinking about what you said about Devon."

"What about it?"

"He really *was* upset with me."

"Well, you did almost get his business license revoked."

"Suspended."

"Whatever. Do you think he did something to the cheese?"

"I don't know," Beckett said. "Probably thought it was karma."

I thought about the man who had put my perishables in the refrigerator for me. Was he capable of murder? "Could he be that mad that he wanted to kill you?"

"I don't know. Maybe just teach me a lesson?"

"And then it went too far?" I asked. "Hmmm . . . that's possible. By the way, where were you earlier? I was looking for you."

"Sitting at home. With my mom and dad. They're so sad. You really don't realize how much you love someone until you can't tell them or be with them."

"I know," I said, thinking about my own dad.

"So, what's next?"

"I'll have to somehow get Officer Callahan to run a drug test on you—you know, your body—if they haven't already. Is that routine? Stephanie said she mentioned to him that you were acting strange. Maybe it's protocol. Maybe he took some initiative."

"Officer Callahan?" Beckett sniffed. "I doubt it. My father said he's lazy."

"Well, I'll see what I can find out." I looked into Beckett's gray eyes. "But I don't know if I can stay here more than a day or two."

"What do you mean?"

"Something's come up. I'll have to get going."

"But you promised me if I helped you with your dog—"

"He's not my dog."

"Sure, he's not." Beckett rolled his eyes. "You *have* to help me. If you don't, wherever you go and whatever you do, I'll . . . I'll *follow* you."

"You've got to be kidding."

"I'm not." He crossed his arms.

Great, from one stalker to another. "I'll do my best, Beckett. That's all I can do."

"All right." He looked at me suspiciously and disappeared.

I let out a heavy sigh. If I didn't solve this mystery in the next day or two, I would be stuck with a sulking ghost at my side for the rest of my life.

And then, of course, there was my money problem—as in, I didn't have much money, which was a problem. I thought of Officer Callahan. Maybe instead of talking to him about Beckett's murder, I should consult him about domestic violence shelters in the area.

As I wondered whether a shelter would allow me to move in with a dog, I turned the corner toward home and nearly ran into a man throwing away fast-food wrappers in a trash can.

"Sorry," I said and then recognized him. He was the guy, Wayne, who had been standing in line in front of me at the register before I darted home.

"No worries," he said just as it began to drizzle. He pulled up the collar of his jacket and walked back to a white SUV parked on the street. In the passenger seat was the woman he had been talking to at Derby's, Cindy. She had a pillow under her head and was trying to snuggle into the seat of the car. A blanket was on top of her.

I stood there, watching her, and an idea hit me like a bolt of lightning. A crazy idea that would probably never work.

But before I could stop myself, I was knocking on the white SUV's passenger-side window.

"Hi," I said when Cindy looked at me, startled. I put my bags down on the sidewalk.

Wayne stepped back out of the car. "I'm sorry, can I help you?" he asked, protectively.

"Well, sorry to bother you, but I was at the market earlier today and was standing in line behind you. I'm not sure if you noticed me."

Wayne and Cindy both shook their heads. *Sure, the one time I want someone to notice and remember me . . .*

"Well, I overheard your conversation—you know, about finding a place to stay—and I think I might be able to help you. My name is . . . Clara. I have a house a few blocks from here. My husband and I own it. It's a very old house and hasn't been lived in for a very long time."

The woman rolled down the window. "I don't understand."

"Your name is Cindy, right?"

Cindy nodded.

"Well, it's just that I thought if you needed a place to crash."

They both looked at me, puzzled. "I don't get it. What's the catch?" the guy said.

"Well, the catch, I guess, is that it's full of dust. And it has no electricity. Just a fireplace. But it's dry, and there's an old mattress that isn't great, but it's better than sleeping in your car. And the toilet and plumbing work. And there's a driveway where you can park." That was the best my sales pitch was going to get.

"Wait, you're offering us your house?" Cindy said, skeptically. "For free? To two total strangers?"

"Well, no, not for free. I'm low on cash, so I thought we could help each other. I was thinking I could charge, like, I don't know, a hundred bucks for the night. Does that seem fair?"

"For a place with no electricity?" Wayne said.

"Wait," Cindy said, intrigued. "You want us to stay with you?"

"Well, I wouldn't be staying *with* you. There's a separate part of the house, a set of rooms that's only accessible from a backdoor. Oh, and it's also accessible through a narrow door in the upstairs bedroom."

"Ah," Wayne said, crossing his arms, "and let me guess, there's a portrait in the bedroom where the eyes have been cut out and you can watch us walk around naked. Or maybe while we're sleeping, you'll use your," he made air quotes, "*secret back door* to rob us blind. Thanks, but no thanks."

I sighed. He was right. This was a dumb idea. "Never mind. I don't know what I was thinking." I picked up my bags. "Sorry to have bothered you."

I kept walking, embarrassed, knowing that Cindy and Wayne were watching me and that I would probably be the star of some TikTok video that was about to go viral. What had gotten into me? *Is this what desperation looks like?* And I had only been on my own for less than a week.

As I got to the intersection where Beckett had been killed, I was about to cross the street when Wayne and Cindy's white SUV pulled up beside me.

Chapter 19

THE SUV BARELY FIT in the narrow driveway, leaving Wayne and Cindy just enough room to squeeze out.

"Well, this is it," I said, pulling out my house keys. It was pretty dark by now, but the streetlights helped me see the key lock.

"It *looks* decent," Cindy said.

"Seriously, Cin?" Wayne asked.

"Is that a dog I hear?" Cindy asked.

"Yeah, that's my dog." I really had to stop saying *my*. "He's a Shih Tzu."

I opened the door and put down my bags. "Give me one minute." I felt my way to the kitchen using the light from the streetlamps, trying not to step on Boy, who was jumping on my legs. I found the flashlight I had stowed in the back of the cabinet and turned it on. "Home sweet home." I shined the light into the main floor of the home.

"Man, you weren't kidding about the dust," Wayne said, stepping in. He had already taken out his phone and was shining his flashlight around. "This can't be healthy."

Or legal, most likely. But I was desperate.

I picked up Boy, who was jumping around Cindy and Wayne, and led them into the living room on the main floor, then upstairs to show them the rest. "It's a lot of room. But like I said, I don't have *anything*. No towels. No clean sheets."

When we got back downstairs, Cindy moved one of the window shades and peeked out a front window. "It's right on a busy street, Wayne."

"You can't seriously be considering this, Cin," Wayne said.

"I can't sleep in the car again, Wayne. I just can't."

"Can you excuse us for a moment?" Wayne asked me.

"Sure." I stepped into the library, holding Boy. I was taking a big risk doing this. What if Cindy and Wayne got hurt on the property and decided to sue? Or contacted law enforcement and had me arrested on the spot? There must be some rule against this sort of thing somewhere.

Wayne stuck his head into the library and shined his flashlight at me. "Hi, Clara? Is that what you said your name was?"

"Yes."

"I'm sorry, you seem like a nice enough person, but this is just a bit too weird for me. You know, your finding us on the street. Standing behind us at the supermarket. Knowing our names."

"You said them. Your names. At the supermarket."

"Yeah, well, I'm a suspicious kinda guy. I'm from New York."

"I totally understand. So am I." I tried to seem empathetic. But I'm sure my face was riddled with disappointment. Cindy seemed like she was still debating whether to take me up on my offer. She was looking around the place, her eyes taking it all in.

"Good luck," Wayne said, "I'm sure that—"

Suddenly, the bathroom door opened wide with a loud creak, startling Wayne and Cindy.

"What was that?" Cindy asked. "Who's there?"

What now? "Oh, it's nothing," I said. *Think of something to say.* "It's just that old houses like this—"

Then the floorboards of the staircase began to creak, slowly, one by one, as if someone was walking upstairs.

Cindy looked at me, wide-eyed. "Is this building haunted?"

"Um . . ."

"Babe, it's a total scam. Gotta be," Wayne said, but there was fire in Cindy's eyes, and she went tearing back up the stairs. Wayne followed behind. I trailed them both, holding Boy.

"The spirit went up here," Cindy said, looking around. "Are you here, spirit? Can you hear me?"

Cindy waited, and then the floor mirror in the corner of the room tilted upward.

"Did you see that?" Cindy said to Wayne, excited. "I told you! I told you the people in my family were gifted. That if we came here, I would be able to communicate with the dead. My mother was able to. So was my grandmother." She looked at me. "We'll stay the night. Wayne, give her the hundred."

"Cin, are you really—"

"Wayne!" Cindy slapped a big kiss on Wayne's lips. "I'll get my stuff. Are my tarot cards in the glove box or in the back? This is even better than that dopey expensive hotel you wanted to book!" She hurried down the stairs. "A haunted house! How fun!"

As Cindy disappeared, Wayne looked at me and shrugged his shoulders. "Well, I guess you've got a deal." He pulled five glorious twenty-dollar bills from his pocket. "I really hope you're for real and not a serial killer."

"I am. I mean, I'm not. I promise." I took the cash. "Let me go down and get my things and leave the two of you alone."

"Where did you say that secret bedroom door was?" Wayne asked.

"Here, I'll show you." I brought him into the bedroom and shined my flashlight along the narrow door in the wall.

Wayne ran his hand along the edges. "You okay with me putting a piece of furniture in front of it for the night?"

"Absolutely. I would do the same."

He nodded and left the bedroom. And just as I started to wonder how I was going to open that secret narrow door, a deadbolt shifted, and the door opened slowly with a creak.

I SPREAD A BLANKET on the floor of the biggest secret room, the one that was adjacent to the upstairs bedroom. It was tough to do in relative blackness since the streetlights were on the other side of the house, but I had my flashlight, and as long as those D batteries still had juice, I was okay.

A few feet away was all the stuff I had dragged in: food for me, food for Boy, one of Boy's toys, my backpack, an additional blanket, and whatever else I could think of. I laid a few wee-wee pads on the other end of the room just in case Boy decided to do me a solid and pee on them instead of the wood flooring.

"May I enter?" William asked from somewhere in the dark.

"Yes."

I picked up the flashlight and shined it around until William appeared in the beam. "That was a big risk, you know," I said. "Moving things around. It might have scared them."

William shrugged. "People possess a fondness for things they do not understand."

"You know, that's what this place is known for, Salem. Ghosts. Hauntings. Witches."

"Is that so?"

I could hear voices in the bedroom through the wall. And then knocking. "Hello?!" Cindy's calls were loud and clear. She must have been talking into the wall. "Are you here, spirit?! I come as a friend!"

"Duty calls," William said and walked through the wall. Moments later, there were excited screams coming from the bedroom, and William stepped back into the beam of my flashlight.

"What did you do?" I asked.

"I toppled the desk chair."

I giggled. "You gave them a thrill. How do you even do that? How do you go invisible so that even I can't see you?"

"I am unsure. It feels akin to closing my eyes." He straightened his coat. "How are you acquainted with such knowledge about Salem?"

"I don't know very much about Salem." I turned the flashlight onto the floor next to me, opened some kibble, and placed it into one of Boy's bowls. Then I poured some bottled water into the other. "I've never been here. I haven't been anywhere, really. Just read about places."

"Likewise."

"Oh, you just reminded me!" I reached into one of my bags and found the magazine I had purchased. "This is for you."

"What might this be?" he asked, surprised.

"It's a magazine. I saw a few on the bookshelves downstairs, so I bought you one. I figured you were tired of reading the same old stuff."

"You procured this for me?"

"It's the least I could do. It's a magazine all about the twentieth century and the first decade of the twenty-first. You can read up on everything that's happened in the past hundred or so years."

His pale, translucent fingers grasped the pages. I was looking for some kind of energy transfer, like static electricity, between ghost and object, but there was none. He somehow interacted with things the way any human would.

"'Tis a gesture of great kindness," he said.

"I hope you enjoy it. And thank you again for your help tonight. I seem to be saying that a lot to you."

"'Tis a pleasure to be of service," William said, flipping the pages. "If you will excuse me . . ."

"Of course. Enjoy."

With that, he nodded and vanished, and the magazine floated to the next room.

I looked at Boy, who had already cleaned his bowl. He came next to me on the blanket, circled a few times, plopped next to my leg, and exposed his belly for me to rub.

"I know this is better than being stuck in a pipe, little one, but this is really no kind of home for you." I rubbed his belly. "You should be snuggling next to a child in a warm bed. Going for long, lazy walks. Playing with other dogs." Boy licked my hand. "I love you, too. And because I do, I think I'm going to have to take you back to the Salem Animal Shelter tomorrow. Maybe Bentley will be able to find you a good home. I'm bad luck. You don't want to be with me."

I took off my wig, lay down on the blanket, and pulled the dog toward me. "But tonight, I'll pretend you're mine. That we'll have many years together of yummy treats and long walks and snuggling under the covers." I ran my hand over that little shaved belly as more knocking came from the wall next to the bedroom.

Give it up, Cindy. No more ghosts in here.

But then the knocking got repetitive and louder, and I realized the sound wasn't Cindy searching for ghosts; it was the bed's headboard banging against the wall.

"Déjà vu, huh?" I said to Boy, whose ears perked up when I spoke. "That bedroom is getting more action today than it's seen in years."

Then I kissed Boy on his wet nose, closed my eyes, and rubbed my compass pendant, praying that neither Wayne nor Cindy got any emergency-room-worthy injuries.

Chapter 20

THE NEXT MORNING, I woke up to daylight. Boy was lying next to me and, to my surprise, so was Ghost Cat, who had curled up between my legs. I carefully maneuvered around them and stood up, pressing my hands into my sore back. Sleeping on the floor wasn't as easy as it used to be in college. I could only imagine what it would be like when I got to Mr. Wiggins's age.

The secret narrow door was open. I figured William had opened it, which meant that Cindy and Wayne must have already left. I walked through the door into the bedroom, where the bed had been made, and it looked like the room had been tidied up. A note was on one of the pillows, along with a Salem postcard. I picked it up.

Clara,

This was one of the greatest experiences of my life! I woke up this morning to find some of our shirts, socks, and things in places other than where we left them. How fun! Thank you so much for sharing your home with us. We're heading back to New York this morning, but I've written my address and phone number on this postcard. Maybe one day we can stay with you again? (Fingers crossed!)

Sincerely,

Cindy (and Wayne)

The odds of Cindy staying with me again were slim to none. I would probably never see her again, and for some reason, that made me sad.

Bark!

Boy was sitting in the secret doorway, staring at me. There was no sign of Ghost Cat.

"I know, I know," I said. "It's breakfast time. For both of us."

Bark!

"Yes, I know. You first."

AFTER I FINISHED FEEDING Boy and put out fresh wee-wee pads for him to avoid peeing on, I quickly had something to eat and got dressed. I needed to wrap up this thing with

Beckett today and get out of the house. I didn't know how fast Rhonda would work her magic, but it was very possible that the cleaning lady person might be at the house as early as tomorrow or the next day. If not sooner.

"William, are you here?"

I waited, but there was no reply. I wondered if he was wandering about the neighborhood. I cleaned up my area in the secret rooms, picking at the last bits of chicken remaining on the rotisserie carcass, and chugged back one of the two cold brews I had picked up at the market the night before. I had to refrain from having another; those things were dangerously addictive, and caffeine was one of the few vices I had allowed myself over the past eight years. Had to stay sharp and one step ahead of Joe at all times.

Boy was gnawing on another dog toy I had bought for him. My heart hurt thinking about having to take him to the Salem Animal Shelter. But if I did, I could return the ridiculous pet carrier, which would give me a little more cash to work with. I started to envision what my life would look like in the immediate future—dumpster diving, sleeping in doorways. I had the urge to call Cindy and ask if I could spend the night at *her* house instead.

"I'll be back soon, little one," I said to Boy, who looked up at me momentarily before ripping off the tag of yet another dog toy.

I checked my burner phone. So far, so good on the charge. I was hardly using it. And I still had a sufficient number of minutes, at least for the next eighty-something days. That was one thing I didn't need to worry about. Just eating and sleeping, the little things.

I turned off the phone and put on my wig. That thing had seen better days, but I didn't have the money to buy another one. I grabbed my house key and phone, stuck them into my pocket, and walked outside.

The sunshine was glorious, and after a night of sleeping on a dusty floor, I sucked the fresh air into my hungry lungs, cleaning out the cobwebs.

"Did you see the local newspaper?" Beckett was standing in front of me.

I was surprised at how not surprised I was by his sudden appearance. I must have been getting used to being surrounded by ghosts. "No, why?"

"I told you. I was right. I was poisoned."

"What do you mean?"

"Do you have internet? The article is on the *Salem Chronicle*'s website. I was reading it over someone's shoulder on the way here."

I took a step closer to Mr. Wiggins's house and turned on my burner. I did a search for the *Salem Chronicle* and found the website, which had a big banner headline:

Salem Track Star's Ketamine Overdose

"It doesn't say you were poisoned. It says you overdosed," I said.

"Exactly! I don't do drugs," Beckett said with a sniff. "Read between the lines."

"Didn't you say you were having parties with underage kids at Derby's and almost got Devon's business license suspended?"

"That was alcohol. Duh." Beckett shook his head. "I would never do drugs. I'd get kicked off the track team. Track is my *life*." He caught himself. "I mean, it *was* my life. Anyway, you have to go in there."

"Go in where?"

"To the *Salem Chronicle*. You have to get them to print a retraction."

"A retraction? Based on what? My talking to Beckett Miller's ghost?"

"I don't know. All I know is I can't have my mother thinking I was a drug addict. It's bad enough I was murdered. Come up with something! You're the private investigator!"

"That's what I keep telling you, Beckett. I'm *not* a private investigator!"

Mr. Wiggins's door suddenly opened, and he stuck out his cheery, wrinkly face. "Oh, hello! Are you calling me, Miss Clara?"

"Oh, I'm sorry, Mr. Wiggins." I must have been yelling. I held up my burner phone. "I was on the phone. I hope I didn't disturb you."

"Not at all," Wiggins said. "I was just watching those nice women on television—you know, the ones who sit around the table and keep interrupting one another." He chuck-led. "I must say, it's nice to hear a friendly voice nearby again."

I didn't know how *friendly* I sounded since I had been screaming at Beckett.

"How are you, my dear?" he asked.

"Oh, I'm good, I'm good. Listen, Mr. Wiggins . . ." I needed to tell him I would be leaving—it was the kind and polite thing to do—but the words weren't coming out. "Well, you see, I'm going to be heading back to—"

"You must come over for lunch next week, my dear. Did I mention I make an excellent chicken tortellini soup?"

"Yes, yes, you did mention that, but—"

"I have so few guests nowadays. So many of my friends and family have passed on. It would be such a pleasure to make dinner for a new friend."

"I . . . I . . ." Ugh. I didn't have the heart to let him down. I would just have to slink away. I was getting good at that kind of thing. "That would be lovely."

A phone began ringing. I could see a phone on the wall in Mr. Wiggins's kitchen.

"Ah, I'd better get that. So many nice young people want to sell me insurance, and I have to let them know I already have more than I need. But my door is always open for you, Clara, if there is anything you need."

"Same, Mr. Wiggins. My door is always open." I smiled. Such a sweet man.

As Wiggins closed his door, Beckett said, "Who still has a landline?"

I glared at him. "Enough, you. C'mon, let's go."

"Where are we going?"

"Where do you think? To the *Salem Chronicle*."

UNSURPRISINGLY, THE OFFICE OF the *Salem Chronicle* was located not far from The Pampered Pup, Derby's, The Haunted Cookie, and every other place you ever wanted to go in downtown Salem. Two large windows with vertical blinds flanked a wooden door with clear glass. I went inside, with Beckett beside me.

An older man was standing at a desk, talking to a young man wearing a button-down, long-sleeved shirt.

"That's Taylor Hampton, the guy in the button-down," Beckett said loudly. I had the urge to shush him, but no one seemed to hear him. "We went to high school together. He was a year ahead of me. He's a jerk. He's had it out for me since day one. He's probably the one who wrote the story."

I pulled out my phone and looked at the article again. Sure enough, the byline had Taylor's name. I typed *Why has he had it out for you* into the web browser and showed it to Beckett.

"Because his younger brother, Clem, and I were in the same grade and on the track team together. Clem sucked at long distances, though." Beckett smirked. "He was more of a sprinter, but for some reason he wanted to run the mile and always came in behind me. Not my fault."

This Taylor guy shuffled some paperwork and handed the man in front of me a receipt. "I'll get this classified in the paper right away, Mr. Hannigan," he said.

"Thank you, Taylor."

"And I hope you find your dog."

I froze. *Dog?*

"You and me both. Mrs. Hannigan is beside herself. We love our little Teddy."

Little?

I felt like I was about to hyperventilate. I had to concentrate to slow down my breathing. Was Boy's real name Teddy? Was this fifty-something man in front of me with the blue denim shirt jacket, gray chinos, and leather boat shoes Boy's daddy? Did Boy own a yacht?

Mr. Hannigan smiled sadly at me as he turned to leave, and I wanted to walk straight to the front desk and let him go without saying anything, but I knew that was wrong on so many levels. 1) I couldn't keep a dog. I could barely worry about myself. 2) If my dog already had an owner, he should be with that owner—even if that owner was negligent enough to leave a gate or door open, letting poor Boy escape and get stuck in a pipe. But the guy seemed heartbroken. And I was many things, but I was no thief.

As Mr. Hannigan reached the front door, I yelled, "Wait!"

He turned his tall frame around. "Yes, young lady?" he asked.

"Did you say you lost a dog?"

"Why, yes, our little Teddy escaped from our front yard. We're not sure how. About three months ago. I had posted signs at the town hall and library, but no one seems to have seen him."

Ugh. Bentley at the animal shelter told me to check those places for signs. I had totally forgotten. In my defense, I did have a lot of things on my mind.

"I thought maybe putting a classified ad in the local paper might help jog someone's memory," Mr. Hannigan said. "Why do you ask?"

"Well, I . . . I mean, a friend of mine found a dog."

Mr. Hannigan brightened. "What does he look like?"

Well, I wanted to say. *He has the most adorable little face. And eyes that peer into your soul. He's so, so smart, too. He already knows his way home, and he likes to play with blond wigs. And he has a best friend who is a Ghost Cat.* But all I could say was, "He's a Shih Tzu, right? Black and white? About three years old?"

Mr. Hannigan's smile disappeared. "No, he's not."

It took everything in me not to jump for joy. "Oh?"

Mr. Hannigan reached into his pocket and took out his phone. He showed me the lock screen. "This is our little Teddy."

I looked at the screen. *Little???* Teddy looked to be a Great Dane, and, when standing on his hind legs, was taller than Mr. Hannigan!

"We miss him so much," Mr. Hannigan said.

"I'm so sorry. I hope he comes home soon."

"So do we." Mr. Hannigan nodded at me and at Taylor and then left the office.

"Can I help you?" Taylor asked when the door closed.

"Ask to speak to Mabel," Beckett said to me. "She's the editor and publisher of the *Chronicle*. You don't want to talk to this clown."

"Oh, um, can I speak to Mabel?"

"Mabel's not here. Is there something I can help you with?"

"Yes," I said, "um . . ."

"Tell him!" Beckett shouted. "Tell him to take down that inaccurate headline!"

"I'm here because of the story you ran on the death of Beckett Miller," I said.

"Yeah, what about it?" Taylor said dismissively as he placed Mr. Hannigan's paperwork on another desk. I was beginning to see why Beckett didn't care for him. You would think Taylor was working for *The New York Times* the way he strutted around the small office. "You want a copy? The print edition will be available tomorrow. Dollar fifty. Five bucks, if you want it signed." He smirked.

"No, I think there's been a mistake," I said.

"I'm afraid not." Taylor rolled his deep-set brown eyes. "Beckett Miller was found with an exorbitant amount of ketamine in his system, according to the toxicology report. A fact is a fact."

"Um," I said, "well, I'm no journalist—"

"Exactly."

"But I didn't think toxicology reports came back that quickly."

Taylor gave an exasperated sigh. "The report is preliminary, which is noted very clearly in my article."

"Not noted very clearly in the headline, though," Beckett said.

"My info is solid," Taylor continued. "My sources tell me the Miller family, who is very influential in Salem, got the coroner's office to act quickly."

"That may be so, but your headline is very misleading," I said. "It says he overdosed."

"An overdose is an excessive and dangerous dose of a drug."

"Yeah, I know what it means, but the word has connotations."

"*Every* word has connotations." Taylor looked at his watch, as if he were bored.

I recognized that smug face. I had slept next to it for eight years. "You don't know how that ketamine got into Beckett's system. You're jumping to conclusions."

Taylor looked at me curiously. "You're being serious?"

"Of course, she's being serious, you idiot!" Beckett screamed.

"Relax," I said.

"I am relaxed," Taylor replied.

"No, I mean . . . it's unethical to—"

"Listen, this is what we're going to press with," Taylor said. "The print edition comes out tomorrow. If you've got a problem with that, I'm going to tell you what I've told everyone else who has called, write a letter to the editor."

The front door opened, and a middle-aged woman in a stylish black coat walked in.

"Oh no," Beckett said, his face softening.

"What is it?" I asked.

"It's my mother."

Chapter 21

Mrs. Miller glanced around the small newspaper office until her eyes landed on Taylor. She squinted, as if scrutinizing a test tube specimen. Or something pesky, like a bug. It wasn't until she took a few steps forward that I realized someone was behind her. Officer Callahan.

"Officer Callahan. Mrs. Miller," Taylor said as if he didn't have a care in the world. "What can I do for you?"

"I think you know exactly what you can do," Officer Callahan said, crossing his arms.

"You're in trouble now, my friend," Beckett said triumphantly.

"I believe you owe Mrs. Miller an apology," Officer Callahan said. "*And* a retraction."

Taylor seemed indifferent, as if Callahan were talking to someone else. "I'm sorry, but I don't make those decisions," he said just as a phone on his desk began to ring.

"I think you'll find that the person who *does* make those decisions is trying to reach you right now," Callahan said.

"Yes!" Beckett shouted. "Nice going, Callahan!" He held up his hand to high-five him, but then pulled back, as if remembering he was dead, when Callahan didn't respond.

"*Salem Chronicle*," Taylor said, picking up the ringing phone. "Yes, Mabel. They're here, but . . . I know, but . . ." He glanced at Callahan. "The article is not incorrect. There's nothing . . . But it *was* an overdose. Mabel, I know you feel as strongly as I do about freedom of the press. That's why you hired me. We can't be bullied into . . . Fine. Yes, okay, that's fair . . . All right. I will. See you tomorrow." He disconnected the call.

"Mabel said she read the coroner's report," Taylor said. "The article stays up."

"You're kidding me," Beckett said.

"But," Taylor continued, "she suggested changing the headline."

"Suggested, huh?" Officer Callahan said.

Taylor looked at Mrs. Miller with no remorse. "I'm sorry for your loss, Mrs. Miller, but the article has been fact-checked and is solid. I am going to change the headline, though. As instructed."

"I don't think you are," Mrs. Miller said, her voice forceful yet serene.

"You don't believe I'm going to change the headline?" Taylor asked incredulously.

"I don't believe you're sorry for my loss," she said and turned her back on Taylor. "Thank you, Officer Callahan. You have been very good to me and my family during this time—fair, as always—which is more than I can say for others." She turned to leave.

"I'm so very sorry for your loss," I said before she reached the door.

Mrs. Miller stopped and searched my face. "Thank you. Did you know Beckett?"

I glanced at Beckett, who was standing beside her and trying to put his head on her shoulder, but it kept falling through. "I did know him. Not very well, but it was obvious to me that he loved you very much. Especially the pancakes you made for him in the shape of a happy face when he came home from school."

A tiny smile appeared on Mrs. Miller's sad face. "What is your name?"

"Clara."

She put her hand on my arm. "Thank you, Clara, for that." She gave my arm a quick squeeze and walked out the door.

"You should be ashamed of yourself, young man," Officer Callahan said to Taylor. "The *Chronicle* has a long and distinguished history in Salem. I've known Mabel Eckers for a long time, and she would never have approved such a sensationalized headline. Perhaps this can be a lesson to you that journalism is not only about information, but the words we use to convey that information."

"Is there anything else you need, Officer Callahan?" Taylor asked with a huff.

"No, I think you've done enough." Callahan looked around the room. "It's a bit chilly in here, you know." He glanced in Beckett's direction without seeing him. "I think the back door or window may be open." Then he nodded at me and walked out of the office. I followed behind. No need to spend any more time with Taylor Randolph Hearst.

As we walked down Hawthorne Boulevard and made a right onto Derby Street, Beckett was quiet. "You okay?" I asked.

He shrugged. "Not really."

"Your mom is strong," I said. "That's where you get it from."

"I don't feel too strong. I feel pretty helpless right now."

"I know. And although you might not believe it, I know what that feels like."

We walked for a little more in silence.

"Man, though, I'd never seen that side of Callahan be-fore," Beckett said, his eyes opening wide with surprise. "My dad said he was always trying to get out of doing his paperwork, so I always thought of him as lazy, but the way he stuck up for my mom was pretty awesome."

"It sure was." I thought about how my dad had always done the same for me. Even when I was wrong. Always stuck by my side. Having a person like that was a gift. I had never taken it for granted. Especially after marrying Joe. "People are complicated."

"So," Beckett said, "the coroner's report."

"Yeah, it looks like there *was* ketamine in your system. How do you think that happened?"

"I don't know."

"Seriously?"

"You don't believe me?"

"I believe you. It's just . . . I would think you'd know if you had been drugged. Did you go out the night before? Maybe hit a few parties?"

"No, I was home. I try to spend as much time as I can with my parents when I'm on break."

I was starting to like Beckett more and more. I should have known better than to think that first impressions are the best impressions. After all, I had been married to Joe. "Okay, and there's nothing like that—you know, ketamine—lying around your house?"

"Drugs? No way. My dad's a cop."

I wanted to say that didn't matter, but I held my tongue. "How long does it take ketamine to cause a reaction or symptoms anyway?" I stopped in front of a coffee shop called The Salem Beanery, which was pretty crowded in-side. I ignored my caffeine cravings and took out my phone, found the open Wi-Fi network, and searched. "Wow."

"What does it say? How long does it take?"

"Not long. Starting maybe at fifteen or twenty minutes to a half hour."

"Fifteen minutes?" Beckett asked, surprised.

"Yeah, and all the stuff you said was happening to you. It's all here." I held up the phone so he could read it. "The dizziness. Vision changes. Confusion. Nausea. It's all in line with a ketamine overdose."

A couple came out of the coffee shop and saw me hold-ing my phone in the air. I smiled and pretended to take a selfie before continuing to walk down the street with Beckett.

"It must have been something you ingested." I tried to remember what Beckett said he ate that morning. "You had your mom's pancakes, right? But that was more than a half hour before you walked to Derby's. You had gone for a run in between. Could it have been the cheese that Devon had out at the deli? Or the donut samples at The Haunted Cookie? Or the chocolates at Haute Chocolate?" Why did Beckett have to eat so much? It was making my job a lot harder. The drug could have been in any of those things. And I was running out of time. I had stuff to pack. A dog to give up. (Gulp.) A life to figure out. (Double gulp.) "What do you think? Beckett?"

We had walked to the corner of the block, and Beckett was staring across the street at Derby's Downtown Market.

"What's the matter?" I asked, following his gaze, and then I saw her.

Maggie.

She was standing in front of Derby's.

Kissing that guy Simon, the one who sold me the cold brews.

Chapter 22

THE KISS DIDN'T LAST long. No sooner had we spotted the pair than Maggie pushed Simon away, appearing less than enamored. In fact, she then slapped him across the face and walked back into Derby's dramatically. Simon appeared apologetic, following quickly behind her.

"My best friend?" Beckett said, bewildered.

"Simon was your best friend?"

Beckett looked at me. "Wait, you know Simon? How?"

"I don't *know* him. He sold me a few of those cold brews."

"Those things taste nasty," Beckett said.

"We're getting sidetracked. What was Simon's relationship to Maggie?"

"There was none. Maggie hated Simon. Said he was annoying. But Simon had a thing for her. Always did. All through school. But she never even looked at him."

I could feel we were onto something. A jolt of electricity ran through me. I was feeling very alive, which made me feel guilty since I was standing next to someone who was very dead. "Tell me again what happened the morning you were killed."

"So you're finally starting to believe I was killed . . ."

"Can you just tell me, Beckett?"

He let out a loud sigh. "I was walking to Derby's . . ."

"Yeah, yeah, yeah, you ate your way through Salem. I know that part. Get to the part where you were *in* Derby's."

"I went into Derby's to talk to Maggie, to let her know I didn't share the photo I had of her. I would never do that. Even if I was drunk." A distant look appeared in Beckett's eyes.

"What is it?"

"Simon knew my password. To my phone."

Another jolt of electricity. "Did he know about the photo?"

"Yeah, I showed it to him."

"How classy of you."

"I know." Beckett hung his head. "Showing off a bit, I guess."

"You think he shared it? So Maggie would get mad at you, maybe, and be with him instead?"

Beckett nodded. "That's possible."

"When was this?"

"During winter break. About four months ago."

"And did Maggie go out with him?"

"No, I told you. She doesn't like Simon. She said he gives her the ick."

Ick . . .

The word sparked a memory. "You know, I heard Maggie on the phone with someone yesterday, and she was getting angry. When she hung up, she said that word. Ick. You think she was talking to Simon? That he was trying to get her to go out with him?"

"Maybe."

"Okay . . ." I started pacing. "So you broke up, and Maggie still doesn't go out with Simon, and he isn't too happy about that. But is that really enough to make him want to do away with you?"

"Wait, there's more."

"There is?"

"I know this might come off as arrogant . . ."

"Why am I not surprised?"

"But I am—*was*—way smarter than Simon. I did everything better. Better grades. Better track stats. The girls liked me more. The two of us were up for a paid internship last year, and I got it. He didn't."

"Did he say he was mad about that?"

"He didn't say anything at all. We didn't really talk about it."

Men . . . if only they talked more. "So he was jealous of you. Was angry that he didn't have the same opportunities or accolades. And when he figured out how to break up you and Maggie, the girl he had always liked, it didn't work, and he still didn't get the girl."

Beckett didn't seem to be listening to me. He was lost in his own thoughts. "I wonder if he was the one who told Devon about my backroom parties?"

"Simon was there?"

"Yeah. I told you. He was my best friend. And if he could get me fired and I was out of the picture, maybe he thought he could get closer to Maggie."

This was a lot of effort for one girl. "But is all this worth killing you for?"

"I don't know. Maybe he just wanted to hurt me."

"You mean physically?"

"Maybe." Beckett's eyes opened wide. "That morning, the morning I died, Simon asked me if I had driven to work. I told him I hadn't, and he had a weird look on his face."

"What do you mean *weird*?"

"Like he hadn't expected me to walk." Beckett began to pace, too. "If he had been planning on drugging me, maybe he intended for me to get into my car and have an accident. Get really hurt. Or hurt somebody else. And then Harvard or the company I was interning with might find out I had drugs in my system, and they would kick me out or fire me."

"Wait a minute . . . You said those cold brew coffees were nasty. You had one of the free samples when you were in Derby's?"

Beckett stopped pacing and looked like he was about to fall down. "I did. And he said he wanted me to have a fresh one, so he went behind his little podium and poured a special one for me."

"Why didn't you mention this when I asked you what you ate that morning?"

"I just didn't think of it as *eating*. I also had orange juice when I had my pancakes, but I didn't think to mention that either. Plus, the cold brew was only a sample. Four ounces. Maybe six? It didn't even register."

"Did it taste weird to you?" I asked. "Different from cold brew coffee?"

"I'm not a coffee drinker, so I—"

"Wouldn't know," we said simultaneously.

That made perfect sense. If Simon had dropped the ketamine in the cold brew, Beckett wouldn't have realized it tasted different because he wasn't a coffee drinker. Truthfully, the cold brew's taste was so strong that *I* might not have even noticed if some ketamine had been dropped in. And because the coloration was so dark, mixing a little something into it wouldn't have been noticeable.

"Wait," I said. "Devon . . ."

"What about Devon?"

"Devon was always watching Simon closely whenever I was at the market. He seems like a nice person, not that that necessarily means anything, but maybe he's involved somehow?"

"I doubt it. Devon is not Simon's biggest fan. He only hired him because I asked him to. And since the whole party-gate episode, Simon's been on probation. Devon has him doing the sample thing sort of as a punishment."

"Why was Simon on probation? If he was the one who ratted you out, why would he implicate himself?"

"I don't know. To throw me off the scent?"

Ooooh . . . that's possible! "So he blamed you for all the things that were going wrong in his life," I said. I had learned there were two kinds of people in the world: those who took responsibility for stuff and those who blamed everyone else. "None of this means anything, though."

"Why not? We have motive. Don't you watch crime shows?"

"Yeah, but it's all speculation. We can't prove anything."

"You know what that means, then." Beckett pulled down on the bottom of his hoodie.

"What does that mean?"

"It means we have to get him to confess."

Chapter 23

"You again?" Simon asked as I stepped up to his little stand. "At this rate, you're going to turn into a coffee bean." He smirked as he held up a container of the shelf-stable cold brew for me to take.

"That's not why I'm here."

"Really?" Simon put the cold brew back on his stand. "Well, I'm not interested. You're not my type. Too old. Have you tried Bumble?"

"Yeah, right," Beckett said next to me. "Like Simon would ever turn down the opportunity to go on a date with *any-one*."

"I'm not interested in that either," I said to Simon, glancing at the deli counter. Where was Devon? The *one time* I needed him to be there. And the market wasn't as crowded as I had hoped it would be. The more eyes and ears, the better, but the aisle was empty. *Relax, you can do this. You had all those years of pretending with Joe.* "What I want to know is, are you trying to kill me?"

"Whoa, lady. What are you talking about?" Simon asked.

"I got sick from your cold brew coffee."

"Don't get mad at me. Take it up with the manufacturer."

"They're not at fault. You are."

"That's impossible." Simon crossed his arms. "You must have gotten sick from something else."

"No, it was you. You tried to kill me," I said. "Just like you killed Beckett."

A small twitch.

That's all it was.

On Simon's right eyelid.

He *did* do it. But a twitch wasn't enough proof. I needed more.

"You have an active imagination," Simon said.

"Not really. My dog's name is Boy."

"Excuse me?"

"I'm not imagining things. You did it."

Simon laughed a little. "So how did I do this, exactly?" he asked. He wasn't folding as quickly as Beckett said he would, begging for forgiveness. Simon may have had crappy grades and couldn't run as fast, but he seemed to have skills Beckett wasn't aware of.

"Keep going," Beckett said to me. "He's gonna break. I can see it in his eyes."

"*You* tell me how you did it," I said, feeling for my phone in my pocket. I knew the recorder was running, but I wasn't confident it would pick up anything other than some rustling. *Please, somebody walk into this aisle!*

Simon looked at me suspiciously. "Did you even know Beckett?"

"Not well, but I know *you* did."

"How do you know that?"

"Beckett told me. He told me you always wanted what he had. That you were a puppy dog who followed him around. That you only got the job here because he got it for you. That you were lucky to be on the university track team at all. And, even with him gone, you can't even get the girl. Maggie won't give you the time of day."

Finally, Simon began to look uncomfortable, and I saw something dark flash across his eyes. "Which is why you killed him," I said, watching him closely.

"How? Apparently, you don't read the papers. Beckett died of a ketamine overdose."

"Because of you."

"No." There was that smirk again. "The guy was a drug addict."

"I was not!" Beckett shouted, stepping behind Simon's counter. "You're a liar!"

"It's what I told Devon in December," Simon said, "when Beckett got fired. How he's been erratic lately. How I was worried about the guy. He was my best friend, after all. First, it was alcohol, those stupid parties, but then he graduated to drugs. Ketamine. Whatever he could find. I wished I could have helped him."

What a performance.

"I think both of us know that you slipped the ketamine into his drink when he came in that morning. You told him you would give him a 'fresh sample,'" I said, using air quotes. "What a guy."

Simon's eyelid began to twitch again. He was probably wondering how I knew that. Unless I had been there or spoken to Beckett before he died, there would be no way.

"It's a great theory." Simon leaned across the stand and peered at me, his brown eyes getting very small. "But just try to prove it."

"I knew it!" Beckett screamed, his pale, gray cheeks flushing with a hint of red. He slammed his hand on Simon's table, and all the little sample cups of cold brew jumped into the air and spilled onto the floor.

"What the—?" Simon said, startled.

"*You* did this to me!" Beckett exclaimed. "You took away my life!" He began pulling packages of coffee off the shelves one by one.

"How are you doing that?" Simon said to me.

I took a step back, probably looking as startled as Simon.

"You were my friend!" Beckett shrieked. "I did *everything* for you! You would have been *nothing* without me!" Beckett raised his arm and swung his fist through the air. It landed on Simon's right cheek, and he fell back onto a metal stand filled with potato chips.

"How are you doing that?!" Simon asked me, his eyes wild with fear. "You're a witch, aren't you?!"

Simon got up and started to run, but Beckett jumped onto his back, and Simon hit the ground again, knocking over a tomato and garlic stand. "Get her off me! Get her off me!" Simon screamed.

He managed to knock Beckett off and got up to run as Beckett chased after him toward the front of the store, where a bewildered Maggie and Beverly—and several customers—were at the registers.

Simon ran out of the exit and onto the sidewalk, but before he could run down the street, Beckett ran *through* the front window and knocked him to the ground. By the time I got outside, Simon was screaming, "Make it stop! Make it stop!"

Beckett was sitting on top of Simon, punching him over and over in the face.

"I'm sorry! I'm sorry!" Simon screamed, holding his hands over his cheeks, his nose, his eyes—wherever Beckett's punches were landing. "Make it stop!"

Beckett didn't stop. Blow after blow. Like a machine. The anger—and what I knew was sadness—spilling out of him.

"Okay, okay, you were right!" Simon said. "I put ketamine in the drink I gave him! You don't understand! Everything came so easy for him! I only wanted to get him kicked off the track team, maybe kicked out of Harvard! I thought he would be driving and get into an accident or something like that! Maybe break his leg! I didn't think he would get killed! I didn't mean to kill Beckett!"

My breath hitched. Beckett stopped hurling punches and fell off Simon's body, which curled into a fetal position as he began to cry. Beckett looked at me, exhausted.

A confession.

A real confession.

But would it matter? It was my word against Simon's.

"We need a police officer right away."

I turned around, and Devon was standing behind me, a phone to his ear. Flanking him were Beverly, Maggie, and a bunch of customers from the store.

They had heard Simon's confession, too.

Chapter 24

Officer Callahan helped Simon, his hands handcuffed, dirty tear tracks lining his face, into the back seat of the squad car. After Callahan shut the door, Simon glanced at me and shook his head, probably wondering what exactly had happened, how a woman he had only seen twice before had somehow gotten the better of him and managed to get him to confess to a crime he thought he had gotten away with.

Callahan and his partner, a cop named Fred Manning, having already gotten preliminary statements from me and the rest of the eyewitnesses, got into the front seat of the car. They drove slowly through a crowd of onlookers who had gathered around Derby's Downtown Market.

"It's usually not this exciting around here."

I turned around. Devon was standing behind me, watching the car go.

"Yeah. And it's only the offseason, right?" I glanced at Beckett, who was standing beside Devon, in front of the store window advertising discounted steak tips.

"What exactly happened?" Devon asked. "With Simon?"

I shrugged my shoulders. "Guilt will do strange things to people."

"Yeah, but those bruises. Did you see them on his face?"

"He probably banged his face on the doors when he ran out of the store. Or on the sidewalk."

"Maybe," Devon said, although I could tell he wasn't buying my explanation. "You're Clara, right?"

"Yeah."

"I saw you talking to Simon on the store's security cameras. You knew him?"

"No."

"It looked like you did. You were arguing."

"As I told Officer Callahan, I came into Derby's to complain about the cold brew he had sold me. I told him he made me sick." *In more ways than one.*

Devon watched me closely. "Something happened to the shelves, too. The coffee samples. They looked like they toppled over on their own. Like they were throwing themselves on the floor."

Okay, smarty-pants, how are you going to explain that one? "I don't know. I didn't see. But I did feel a draft. Maybe it was the wind from an open door somewhere."

"And I could have sworn Simon was yelling, 'Get *her* off me.'"

"Yeah, that was weird. I heard that, too. But I'm sure you could see that I wasn't anywhere near him." I shrugged. "I just don't know."

"Hmmm," Devon said, thinking. "Well, I'd better get inside and settle everyone down. I'm sure Beverly has already posted on social media and has got the whole town talking. Derby's Downtown Market in the news once again." He shook his head. "Have a good day, Clara."

"You too," I said, watching him go.

"Devon's a good guy," Beckett said. "It's funny. I feel like I've aged years since last December when he fired me. I should have never thrown those parties in his backroom. What was I thinking?"

"You probably weren't. You were young."

"Yeah, well, maybe now with me gone—and Simon, too—Devon can get on with the business of running the market." Beckett looked at the onlookers who had begun to disperse. "It could have been the perfect crime, you know. Most of these people here probably thought I *did* overdose. Lucky for me, I met up with an amazing amateur sleuth."

"I don't know if I would call myself a sleuth."

"That's exactly what you are. Simon would have gotten away with it all if it wasn't for you, Clara. Thank you for believing in me."

"I had no choice. You threatened to stalk me for the rest of my life." I smiled.

"I did do that, didn't I." He laughed. "Sorry about that."

"Nah, it made me realize how determined you were. And also how innocent. Guilty people don't go out of their way to save a little dog to get someone to help them prove their innocence." Or did they? I had no idea.

"I don't know how to repay you."

"To be honest, it felt good to be able to do something important and helpful for somebody. For a long time, I've felt trapped and felt like I was no good to anyone. I should be thanking you for reminding me of why I couldn't stay where I was."

"Looks like we're both free now."

"I guess so. How do you feel?"

"I feel . . . different," Beckett said. "More at peace." He glanced up at the sky. "I think it's time for me to go."

"How do you know?"

"I don't know," he said. "I just know." He held out his hand.

I reached out my hand and felt Beckett's fingers curve around mine in a handshake, our palms touching, my pink skin to his gray. "Looks like you figured out this crossing realms thing in the nick of time."

"You were right, I guess," he said. "When I stopped thinking about it, it happened."

I shook his hand. "May you rest in peace, Beckett Miller."

"Thanks to you, Clara Kelly, I will." Then he slowly faded away until my outstretched hand was empty.

I HURRIED HOME, WHERE Boy was waiting dutifully for me by his food bowls, wagging his curly little tail.

"It was a good day for us, Boy." I quickly poured some kibble and fresh water into his bowls. "We did it. We solved the mystery." He jumped up, his little paws on my shins, and gave my hand a quick lick. "I know," I said. "We make a good team."

As I watched him eat, my mood went from light to heavy. I had done what was right for Beckett. But now I needed to do what was right for Boy, too. A life on the road was tough for a person, let alone a pet. Just because I was running didn't mean Boy should have to. After he finished eating, I put on his harness, attached his leash, and we walked to the Salem Animal Shelter.

When we got there, I picked up Boy and peered inside the window. Bentley was playing with one of the dogs. He saw me and waved. He scooched the dog back into a cage, walked toward me, and opened the front door. I stepped inside.

"Hi there," Bentley said. "It's a little quieter than the last time you were here, I'm happy to say." He smiled. "The dogs have all been fed, had a little exercise, and now they're taking a siesta. I need one myself." He laughed. "And I'm happy to say we've had an adoption! That's always a good day." He petted Boy's head as Boy's tongue feverishly tried to lick his hand. "Did your friend have any luck finding the dog's owner?"

"Um, about that."

"Your little guy is so cute." Bentley smooshed his face. "Seems like a happy dog."

"He is. Very happy."

"Sorry, what was that you were saying? About your friend? They found the dog's owner?"

"Actually, no, she hasn't."

"And no chip, right?"

"No, no chip."

"Well, I guess she has two choices. She can either keep the dog or she can certainly bring the dog here. People come in all the time looking for little dogs. I wish I could say the same for some of these guys." He motioned inside the shelter. "Not many people want to adopt a big dog or an older dog. It takes a special kind of person. What I try to do is give these dogs as good a home as I can while they're with me."

"You're a kind man, Bentley."

He smiled. "We all do what we can, right? What do you think your friend wants to do?"

"Well," I said, "I think—"

The door to the shelter opened, and a man came rushing inside. I recognized him—Mr. Hannigan, the person who lost his dog.

"Where is he? Where is he?" Mr. Hannigan said, breathless. "Where's my boy?"

Bentley's face burst into a smile. "He's right here, Mr. Hannigan. Hold on one moment." Bentley hurried to the back of the shelter and returned with a giant dog, one that was quite possibly part horse and was pulling hard on its leash.

"Teddy!" Mr. Hannigan exclaimed, prompting Bentley to drop the leash.

The dog leaped into Mr. Hannigan's arms, nearly toppling him over. "Oh, boy, I've missed you so much!"

"You found him!" I said to Bentley.

"A sweet couple brought him in this afternoon," Bentley said. "Apparently, he was near one of the buildings over by the yacht club."

"Teddy, were you looking for me to go sailing?" Tears were streaming down Mr. Hannigan's face. "Life just wasn't the same without you, buddy."

"I have the names of the couple who brought him in, Mr. Hannigan." Bentley went to the counter and returned with a piece of paper. "If you want to get in touch."

"I'll do that." Mr. Hannigan placed the big dog's front paws back on the ground and took the paper from Bentley's hand. "Thank you, Bentley." He picked up the leash and opened the door. "Let's go see Momma, Teddy!" he said, and the two hurried out of the shelter.

"A happy ending," Bentley said.

"Those are the best kind."

"So," Bentley said, "you were saying about your friend's dog . . ."

My heart was pounding, and I wiped the tears that had formed in the corners of my eyes while watching the reunion of Mr. Hannigan and his beloved Teddy. "Yeah, well . . . I think she—my friend—is . . . going to keep the dog after all." I fiddled with Boy's bowtie clip. "She's sort of fallen in love with him. I think it's taken her a long time to admit that to herself. She thought that she would be able to do things alone. That she was better off being alone. But I think she finally realized she isn't, that there's no way she would be able to part with the little guy. That love is the most important thing, no matter what. And the rest, they'll figure out together."

"Well, that sounds lovely." Bentley's eyes glanced at Boy. "If she ever needs any help with anything, you tell her to call me."

"I will," I said, walking out the door.

I placed Boy on the sidewalk, but when I turned to walk down the street, I ran right into someone heading into the shelter.

"Oh, my gosh, excuse me. I'm so sorry," I said and found myself looking into a familiar pair of green eyes. "No way. Not again."

"You really have to stop making a habit of bumping into people," Sebastian said with a laugh, resting the brown shopping bag he was carrying on the sidewalk. "Where were you going in such a hurry?" He spotted Boy. "And, hey, you have your little buddy with you. I'm guessing you decided to keep him?"

I glanced back at Bentley, hoping he didn't hear, although I had a feeling Bentley knew there was no "friend" who found a dog. Bentley was already in the back of the shelter, letting an older dog out of his cage to sit on his lap. I wished I could take all the dogs with me.

"Yeah, I don't think I can part with him," I said.

"I knew the minute I saw you two that you were a match made in heaven," Sebastian said.

"Well, then I guess I'm one for two in the relationship department."

"Sorry?"

Did I just say that out loud? "Never mind. I'm actually glad I ran into you, Sebastian. I wanted to thank you again, before we left, for what you did for Boy this week."

"You're leaving?" Sebastian asked, frowning. "That's too bad."

Don't look into those green eyes. Don't do it! "Yeah." I moved Boy's leash to my other hand and stuck out my right hand, trying to concentrate on Sebastian's eyebrows, his nose, the little freckle he had on his forehead—anywhere but those eyes. "It was really good to meet you."

Sebastian shook my hand. "It was good to meet you, too, Clara. May the two of you have lots of great adventures." He lifted the shopping bag with his other hand. "Well, I'd better get these cleaning products to Bentley."

"Still paying it forward, I see."

"Always." Sebastian gave my hand one last squeeze before going into the shelter, leaving me on the empty side of a handshake for the second time that day.

WHEN WE GOT HOME, Boy ran off to play with one of his toys, and I immediately started gathering my things before I lost my nerve. Salem was beginning to feel too much like a home, and I couldn't let that happen. Rhonda's cleaning woman would be here any day now. I needed to go, and with the extra money I got from Cindy and Wayne, I probably had enough to buy a bus or train ticket to . . . well, *somewhere*. Did buses and trains allow pets? No clue. Maybe I could say Boy was my emotional support animal. Which wasn't a lie. He certainly had supported me plenty over the last three days.

I shoved some toiletries into my backpack and saw the hair dye. I had forgotten all about it, but I had no time to take care of that now. Maybe at my next stop. *Wherever that was.* I touched the top of my head. Luckily, Boy hadn't completely destroyed my blond wig.

As I collected garbage for disposal and packed my clothing and gadgets as well as Boy's things, I started thinking about all the places we could go. The adventures we could have, as Sebastian had said. I needed to focus on the positive. Maybe we would travel to the Midwest. Or somewhere else in New England. Like New Hampshire. I had always wanted to see New Hampshire. It was where my dad's family had come from.

I was beginning to feel more positive, despite the odds against me. Maybe I could find a shelter or a church that could help us. Despite what had happened to Beckett, my short time in Salem had gotten me feeling better about people. Like Officer Callahan. Bentley. Sweet, old Mr. Wiggins. And green-eyed Sebastian. There were nice folks in this world. I just had to find them.

Meow!

On the middle of the staircase, Ghost Cat was rubbing her little head against one of the balusters, watching me. I smiled and walked over, placing my hand near her little faded head. She pushed into my palm, the gray fur brushing against my skin.

"Goodbye, little one. Take care of William."

William.

I needed to tell him I was leaving. I didn't want to just slink away like I was doing with Mr. Wiggins. But something told me the conversation would be one of the hardest I'd ever have in my life. William was my friend. The only one I had these days. I didn't know what to say. I decided to finish packing up all my stuff before calling for him. It would give me some time to think. Or maybe I was just procrastinating.

"Okay, Boy, I think I left some of your dog toys upstairs in the secret rooms."

Boy ran toward the staircase. *Such a smart dog.* He put his little paws on the first step.

"You want to come with me, you cutie?" I picked him up, kissed his little head, and hurried upstairs.

I checked the bathroom and the little bedroom with the frilly bed, which was all tidied up. None of my clothing or Boy's things around. The larger bedroom was mostly in order, too. I held Boy with one hand and adjusted the desk chair under the desk. Everything seemed just as it was when I arrived.

The narrow wall door was ajar, and I carried Boy into the secret rooms. Sure enough, Boy's favorite stuffed toy, the woolly mammoth, was on the floor.

"Aha!" I said. "We can't leave without this. I paid way more than I should have for it." I picked it up and placed it into my pocket, and as I walked back through the narrow door into the bedroom, Boy started to growl. A low, vibrating sound, like the hum of an air conditioner.

Weird. I had never heard him growl before.

"What is it, Boy?" I said when there was a noise at the other end of the room.

I looked up and froze.

Joe was standing in the doorway.

Chapter 25

MY HEART POUNDED AGAINST my rib cage as I held Boy tightly in my arms.

"Did you really think I wouldn't figure out where you were, Emily?"

Joe looked different. Smaller than I remembered. Like he had diminished in stature. Maybe some distance had given me a new perspective. For years, I had wondered what I had seen in him when we met. I had been taken in by a good-looking exterior, which hid his ugly inside. Now the inside was all I could see.

Still, I knew he was dangerous. But I stared directly into his eyes, something I tended to avoid throughout my marriage. I would always back down. Never challenged him. Because of my father. Because I didn't want to rock the boat while I was stuck there. But I wasn't that scared girl trying to protect her father anymore. I had no one to protect. "Leave me alone, Joe. I mean it."

"Oh, you mean it, huh?" He waved his hands in the air, jazz-hands style. "Oooh, scary."

He took a step into the bedroom and looked around like he hadn't just been in there the day before, banging his realtor. "I always knew this place would be worth hanging onto one day. I'd ask how you got in, but I'm assuming, since there didn't seem to be any signs of a break-in, that you had managed to copy the key." He clapped his hands. "Bravo. I underestimated you."

Grrrrrr . . .

"What's with the dog?" he asked.

Oh no. The dog.

I *did* have something to protect.

"He's not mine," I lied. "I'm watching him for a friend." Joe needed to believe Boy belonged to someone else because then he wasn't likely to hurt him. That's what he did. Found your weak spots. The things and people you loved the most. I knew he would have no trouble hurting my dog. I had seen him hurt animals before.

"Watching for a friend, huh? You never were a good liar, Emily. I have to say, though, you skipped town faster than I thought you would. Took me by surprise. I thought you'd want to take care of the arrangements for your father."

"He had everything in place already. Nothing to take care of."

"Ah, the two of you were a team, huh? Conspiring to-gether? This way, when your father crossed the rainbow bridge, you could run off into the sunset and get away from your no-good, awful husband." He smiled. "Lucky for me, I wasn't about to miss the most important tech conference of the year just because you decided to play hide-and-seek. I knew I'd find you eventually, but who knew I'd find you so fast? Even *I* didn't think you were stupid enough to run away to the very place I was supposed to visit." He laughed. "I could smell you the moment I got here, like a month-old trash heap. Plus, the footprints? The ashes in the fireplace? It wasn't rocket science. I played it cool, though, didn't I? Got rid of Rhonda. I knew you'd still be here when I got back. You always thought you were smarter than me." He squinted at me. "But, seriously, what's with the blond contraption on your head? Is that supposed to fool me?" He laughed again. "Where were you hiding when I was getting it on with Rhonda here in this room? In that secret room there?" He pointed to the narrow door.

I stood silently as Boy growled again.

"That little rat seems to want to protect you. How quaint." He cracked his knuckles, an annoying habit. "Now, I'm going to explain what's about to happen, Mrs. Turner. You're going to go into my car quietly."

"I am not."

Joe put his hand up as if to shush me. "You are going to get into my car, Emily."

"I'll scream."

"Go ahead, scream, but I'm not sure who's going to hear you. That old man next door who can barely see out of his face slits? And even if someone did, say, hear you, it wouldn't be enough time to save that dog of yours that you claim isn't yours."

I inched toward him when everything in me wanted to run and hide. I needed to stand up to him. One small step for me. One giant leap for the rest of my life. "You will not touch a hair on this dog's head."

"Is that a threat? You think just because your pathetic father died, I can't control you."

Suddenly, Joe charged toward me, but as I grabbed Boy tightly and tried to run, William appeared in front of me. He held out his arms, elbows first, and Joe ran into them, stumbling backward.

"You will refrain from laying hands upon her, sir," William said. "I would like for you to leave."

Joe lay on the floor, dazed. "How did you do that, Emily?" he asked with a laugh, rubbing his jaw, then wiping the dust from his hands. "Is that a new trick you've learned while you've been away from home?"

"That wasn't a home," I said. "It was a jail."

"Po-*tay*-to, po-*tah*-to." Joe was feeling around on the floor, as if looking for some kind of tripwire. He got up and jerked his body toward me, making me flinch. He laughed again. Then he tried coming at me head first, like a battering ram, but William stood firm, and Joe's head bounced off William's hands, and he tumbled to the floor again.

I could tell he was hurt and trying to shake it off. He wasn't laughing anymore.

"What is this, Emily?" Joe glared at me. "What are you doing?"

Then I realized: Joe couldn't see William. Or hear him.

"Go away, Joe," I said as William went to the other side of the room and lifted the desk chair high in the air.

I didn't know if I expected Joe to run at the sight of a floating piece of furniture or not, but he didn't. He stood up and watched the chair closely. "How are you doing that, Emily? Are you a witch? You came to the right place, it seems."

William moved the chair closer to Joe, at a threatening angle, and I suddenly remembered what he told me. How he had promised himself long ago never to harm another—a promise that must have had something to do with the war and why he was here, haunting this old house. Did he intend to break that promise to protect me? If so, I couldn't let him.

"You think some parlor trick is going to get me to back off?" Joe asked. "Do you have a ghost bodyguard or something?"

William raised the desk chair higher in the air.

"Don't do it, William," I said.

"William, is it?" Joe asked.

"He's not worth it, William," I said.

"So you've been shacking up with a ghost, huh? What a step down from me." Joe took another step toward me, but William carried the chair and placed it between us.

"I say again, I would prefer you to leave," William said to Joe.

"It's cute, Emily, how you think a chair is going to keep me from what I want, how you think you've won. Didn't you learn anything about me in all the time we've been together? I never lose. Never." He stabbed his hands in the air and waved them around, like he was doing the hokey pokey, as if trying to find William in the room. "I never lose," he said again. "Not to any man, alive or otherwise." Then he looked directly at me. "And certainly not to a woman."

Joe dodged around the chair at me, but William stepped in the way. When Joe threw a punch, it went right through William, who grabbed him by the neck and tossed him to the floor.

"I feel embarrassed on your behalf, sir," William said, his voice angry for the first time. "What my shame has brought on you."

Joe wiped the dust off his hands again. "You don't want to leave, Emily? Fine. You know what? You don't have to. You and your paranormal lover can die here for all I care. Hauntedly ever after." He smiled wickedly. "I'll put a match to this place."

He must have seen my jaw drop slightly because his eyes widened. He had found it. My weak spot. The chink in my armor. "Fires happen in old, abandoned buildings all the time, don't they?" He began backing away.

I couldn't let Joe take William's house away from him. Would the local fire department get here in time? Maybe. But what about all of William's books? Where would he go if the whole place burned down? He had lived here for so long. "I'll go with you, Joe."

But Joe had fire in his eyes. He sensed he had the upper hand. I knew that look well. "It's too late," he said, and I knew he would do it. Just to spite me. Even if he lost money. He would burn down his own house just to hurt me.

"I found a matchbook downstairs," Joe said. "Old, dusty thing, but I'm sure it'll do the trick." He ducked out of the doorway.

"Joe, wait!" I shouted. "Joe!"

"It's all right, Clara," William said.

"No, it's not!"

I ran after Joe as he bounded toward the staircase.

"You'll come back to me after all, won't you, Emily! You'll never escape me. Never!" Joe shouted as he grabbed hold of the banister. But as he was about to run down the stairs, he tripped and fell, tumbling head-first down the long, narrow stairwell, crying out in pain until there was no sound at all.

I ran to the top of the staircase and looked down. Joe was lying at the bottom, unmoving, his head cocked at an unnatural angle, his body splayed below him.

"My word!"

A voice.

I thought it was William when Mr. Wiggins popped into view on the first floor. *What was he doing here?* He looked up at me. "Are you all right, my dear?" he asked.

I barely heard him. My head was spinning. And my attention was focused elsewhere—on the top step of the staircase, where Ghost Cat was lying, rubbing her furry, pale head against the wood baluster.

Chapter 26

"We meet again, Clara Kelly."

Officer Callahan pulled out a chair from the dining room table and sat with me as I watched the paramedics wrap Joe in a black body bag.

"Hello, Officer Callahan," I said, holding tightly onto Boy.

"I'm sorry, but I'll need to get a statement, Mrs. Kelly. I've already spoken to Mr. Wiggins, but I'd like for you to explain exactly what happened here."

What to say? *My abusive husband tripped over a Ghost Cat on his way to burn down this building?* My mind was reeling from all the lies and half-truths. For eight years, I had been white-lying my way through my marriage, all to keep myself and my father safe. To keep things status quo while I figured out my next move. But if I really wanted to start a new life—if that had been my intention for coming here—then that had to stop. An authentic life required truth. Well, as much truth that wouldn't make me seem like I was a ghost-whispering crazy person. I had to ease into my new authentic life, slowly freeing myself from the shackles of my old one. I took a deep breath.

"When I came home today after stopping at the Salem Animal Shelter, my husband showed up, surprising me when I was upstairs."

Callahan looked around. "It seems to me like you were packing."

"I was. My time here had come to an end. And I was upstairs seeing if any of my dog's toys had been forgotten."

Callahan indicated the backpack. "You pack lightly, Mrs. Kelly. Not many clothes."

"No. I hadn't expected to stay here for more than a few days."

"You said you were surprised to see your husband. Why?"

"He had attended a tech conference in Boston and stopped by yesterday with his realtor, Rhonda Hooper. I didn't think he would be back. I thought he was heading home."

Callahan nodded. I was sure Wiggins had mentioned he had seen Joe yesterday. "Why did he come back?" he asked.

I wasn't sure how much Mr. Wiggins had heard. "Joe wanted to talk with me."

"What about?"

"Getting rid of this house." That was one way of saying *arson*.

"I take it you weren't on board with that decision?"

"No, I wasn't. Since I've been in Salem, I have taken a liking to the area. I wanted to keep things as they were. The argument got heated. And then he stormed toward the stairs and fell. I was in the bedroom. By the time I got to the top of the staircase, he was at the bottom of the stairs, lying still."

"But you weren't the one to call 911?"

"No. Kind Mr. Wiggins said he would."

"Do you know why Mr. Wiggins was here?"

"I didn't at first. But after he called the ambulance, I came downstairs, and he sat me down. Right here." I motioned to the chair I was sitting in. "I don't think I've moved since. Mr. Wiggins told me why he had come. He had heard us arguing—Joe had left the front door open, and Mr. Wiggins was disposing of some trash. He came inside to see if I was all right and that's when Joe fell."

Callahan nodded. "He said he heard you run from the bedroom." He looked at me closely, reminding me of the way I had been scrutinizing Simon. Looking for tells. For signs of deception. "It seems to have been a terrible accident."

I didn't know whether to nod or speak or look into Officer Callahan's eyes. I just continued petting Boy's head.

"If you don't mind my saying so, Mrs. Kelly, you don't look at all upset about the loss of your husband."

"I'm not a doctor," I said, "but I think I might be in shock."

Officer Fred Manning walked into the room. "I think we're done here, Carl," Manning said.

"I think so." Callahan closed his notebook and stood up. "Thank you for your time, Mrs. Kelly. If anything should come to you, please don't hesitate to contact me."

"I will, Officer Callahan. Thank you."

Callahan began to walk toward the front door and stopped. "Please don't take this the wrong way, Mrs. Kelly, but I'm hoping I won't be seeing any more of you in the near future."

"Agreed," I said.

"My condolences for your loss."

When Callahan closed the door, I leaned back in my chair and let out a big sigh. I had done the right thing. I hadn't lied to Callahan. I didn't tell him the entire truth, but I didn't lie. Baby steps. And I really did think I was in shock.

"Permission to enter?" William's voice said.

"Yes, of course, William."

William appeared near the doorway to the library. Boy was struggling to get off my lap, and when I put him down, he ran to William, trying to jump up on his legs but landing on the floor, confused.

"Is Joe really gone?" I asked.

William moved closer to me. "What is your meaning behind those words?"

"I keep wondering if Joe is still here. What if he suddenly appears, like you? As a ghost. What if he haunts me for the rest of my life?"

"I believe your husband's spirit has moved on."

"How can you be sure?"

William straightened his jacket. "I have witnessed this afore. His life bears no incompletion. He brought about his own demise. Such was the way of all the men who lived in this house. I have witnessed the passing of many unkind, yet complete lives. And each time, their spirit crossed over."

"But you're still here?" I said.

"I am."

"Why?"

William was quiet.

"I know we said we wouldn't talk about our past, but sometimes by talking about it, we can figure out the future," I said. "I'm thinking maybe I can help you to . . . um, cross over. Like I helped Beckett Miller." He seemed to ponder this. "Do you think you're here because you feel responsible for the sins of your descendants?"

"Perhaps. Although I suspect there are other reasons as well." William's attention was suddenly elsewhere. He was staring at the living room. "You may," he said.

I followed his gaze. "Who are you talking to?"

"Someone has asked to come in and see you. I've invited him in," he said before vanishing.

"I don't understand," I said into the empty room. Boy was sitting near the front windows, also staring at something. I got up and slowly walked toward the living room. When I peered inside, I gasped.

Chapter 27

"Daddy!" I yelled.

My father's ghost was standing in the middle of the room, smiling at me. I tried throwing my arms around him, but I was unable to. He seemed to be trying to do the same.

"It takes some time to figure out," I said. "That's okay. It's just so good to see you."

"My Emily," he said.

He didn't look sick, the way his body had shriveled toward the end. He looked like the daddy I knew and loved.

"You're here," I said.

"And you're safe." He glanced with interest at my hair.

"Oh, this thing." I reached up and pulled off my blond wig, letting my long red tresses fall to my shoulders.

Bark!

Boy was sitting at attention next to me, looking at the wig with enthusiasm.

"Here, Boy, you want it? It's all yours." I threw it to him, and he greedily snatched it up and ran toward the fireplace, which seemed to be his favorite spot in the house.

"That's my dog," I said.

"I see that."

"How did you know where I was? How did you find me?"

"I don't know. I had been searching for you. Unable to rest. Something inside me," he pointed to his midsection, "seemed unsettled. Someone by the name of William found me. A polite fellow. Military man. I can't even tell you where I was at the time. Or how he knew who I was. He told me where you were and how to get here."

William left the house? To help me?

"I'm so glad he did." I took a deep breath. "Joe is dead, Daddy."

"I know."

"How?"

"I'm not sure. Like a pain I've felt for a very long time subsiding." He looked around the room, at the many books on the shelves. "When I was outside this house, I heard the officers talking about you. They called you Clara Kelly."

I nodded. "When I ran away from Joe, I wanted to start over. And I thought I'd start with a new name."

"Good choice. It suits you." He looked at me as he used to, with pride and love, his caring face reminding me of a childhood filled with happy memories. "I carried such guilt thinking you were trapped in that horrible marriage because of me."

"Daddy, please." I tried to reach for his hand. "I made my choices. Bad ones, for sure. But they were *mine*. You just got caught in the middle." I smiled but could feel the tears forming in my eyes. "Daddy, can I ask you a question?"

"Of course, pumpkin."

"Is that why you didn't get treatment for the cancer? You didn't want to give me a reason to stay in my marriage?" I couldn't bear the thought of my father choosing death over life because of me.

"Emily, you must never think that way. My cancer was very aggressive and had progressed so much. I thought long and hard about my decision. It would have been a terribly uphill battle. I didn't want to live the last months of my life on a hospital bed. I wanted to spend as much time as I could with you. Thank you for making those months wonderful. I still hum the songs from that Earth, Wind & Fire concert." He turned serious. "Although sometimes I do think I opted not to get cancer treatment because . . . well, I miss your mother, and maybe a part of me wanted to see her."

"I miss her, too, Daddy."

"I wish she could see you now. All grown up. Able to do all the things you want. Have a career. Travel. See the world." He looked at Boy. "Have a dog. Be who you were meant to be. Now I know that we will all be with each other again someday." He tried reaching for my hand. "I think it's time for me to go now, pumpkin. I feel . . ."

"Free?" I thought of Beckett.

"Yes. Untethered. This is no longer my world. It's yours. And you are free to live your life now as you see fit."

"I love you, Dad."

"I love you, too . . . *Clara*." Then my father glanced at the compass pendant around my neck, smiled, and disappeared.

Chapter 28

I PULLED MY NEW car into the narrow driveway and stared
at the front door. Had it really been three months since I'd
first come to Salem? I imagined myself standing there on the
doorstep, wet, alone, and afraid.

Bark!

"Yes, I know, Boy." He was wagging his tail, eagerly waiting for me to unclip him from his seat belt restraint. He had
his front paws on my books, which were piled next to him.
Two of favorite things. My Boy and my books.

I downed the rest of my Starbucks Grande and got out
of the car. By the time I got to the back passenger side, Boy
had his paws on the window, his little breath fogging up the
glass. I opened the door, scooped him up in my hands, and
walked up the cracked steps, sticking my key into the lock.
Mr. Wiggins's door was open behind me, and I could see him

talking with Mrs. Birchgirdle. It looked like they were having warm tea and warm conversation. I thought about saying hello but didn't want to disturb them. How wonderful it was they had found each other.

I opened the door and placed Boy on the floor. He ran right into the library as I began to look around. Everything was just as I had left it. I glanced at the bottom of the stairway, where Joe's body had been. There was no sign of it now. No sign it had ever been there. A new, light layer of dust covered the floor.

In the living room, Boy was sniffing around the bookshelves. I ran my hand along the books' spines, remembering my plan to plop down in the room's chair and read them all.

"May I come in?"

I had hoped to hear William's voice. "Of course," I said.

He appeared near the fireplace. "Why, Clara, you look . . . lovely." He was looking at my freshly washed red hair.

"Thank you. You don't look so bad yourself. How are you?"

"I am faring adequately, thank you."

I couldn't help but smile. That was such a William thing to say. I sat down on the plastic-covered sofa. "I'm so sorry to have rushed out of here that night. I think . . . well, that I just needed to think."

"I assume you have been quite busy." William stepped toward the bookshelves.

"It's been overwhelming. I drove Joe's car back to our house on Long Island. So strange being back there. It never really was my home. Joe grew up there. Knew all its nooks and crannies. The first thing I did was get rid of all those damn cameras. At least the ones I knew about. Then I went to see Joe's parents. And his sister."

William was listening intently. To my every word.

"I find myself in an unusual situation. All of Joe's assets—his property and stock holdings—have passed to me. Joe didn't have a will. I think he expected to live forever. In fact, I'm sure he did. And I'm pretty sure he didn't want *anything* to go to me, but under New York State laws, if the deceased is survived only by a spouse, no children, then that spouse inherits everything."

"You have earned such an inheritance, Clara."

"Part of me agrees with you. And part of me doesn't want it. Joe's parents divided their properties between their two children, Joe and his sister. You can imagine that they're not too happy with the idea of me inheriting buildings and legacies that have been in their family for generations."

"Are you happy?" William asked.

I took a deep breath and exhaled. "That's a good question. Lord knows I've dreamt of Joe disappearing from my life for many years, and then when it happened, I was a bit lost. Not sure of which way to go."

"Clara Kelly, you now have the capacity to pursue all that you have long desired," he said. "You are at liberty to explore the world."

I peeled back the corner of the dusty furniture cover and ran my hand along the fabric underneath. "I know. But it's a funny thing, William. I've spent so much time wanting to run, so much time trying to figure out how to get away from Joe, that I never really focused on where or what I was running *to*."

"I don't understand."

"Coming here . . . meeting you . . . well, it changed my life." I stood up. "I was so busy running away from home that I guess I didn't realize I may have *found* my home."

I suddenly felt nervous. I had been working up the courage the entire car ride from New York to say what I wanted to say, but now that I was here, the words were getting caught in my throat. William didn't say anything. Just watched. And listened.

"I was thinking . . . um . . . well, if it's all right with you, I thought I could come here to live. I thought I could, you know, fix the place up. Maybe turn it into some kind of bed-and-breakfast or Airbnb. What do you think? I know a little bit about the hotel industry, and I've already had some practice with Cindy and Wayne, right?" I smiled. "When we have guests, I can stay in the secret rooms with Boy. Use the back entrance to come and go."

"What about traveling? Seeing the world?"

"There's always time for that. For the first time in a very long time, I get to decide what I want to do and when. Make my own decisions. Start again. I've thought long and hard about it. This is what I want. To stay here. With you."

I saw movement out of the corner of my eye as Ghost Cat entered the room. She curved her body around one of the legs of the sofa and walked straight to me, rubbing against my shin. Boy spotted her and pounced toward her.

Bark! Bark!

Ghost Cat ignored him and walked through the wall into the other room, but Boy went scrambling after her, undeterred.

"Quite the interesting pair," William said.

"Yes." I took a step toward him. "William, you've lived here a long time. And it's been quiet. And Lord knows a bed-and-breakfast will be noisy, filled with all kinds of people. Children. Pets, even. And you see how much noise Boy can make. And I know it must not be fun to have to announce yourself all the time in your own home just to come into a room that I'm already in, but it might be nice to have somebody to talk to. I know it will be for me." I stopped talking. I knew William was too polite to interrupt me.

"You wish to control your," he thought for a moment, "destiny? You wish to remain here?"

"Yes. Very much. How do you feel about that?" I didn't want to pressure him. "Do you want to think about it?"

William straightened himself and adjusted his jacket. "No need to think. I should like that very much," he said, his pale blue eyes twinkling.

"Really?"

"Indeed."

"Then we have a deal." I stuck out my hand.

William eyed it curiously, and I wondered if he had ever shaken hands with a woman before. He reached his hand toward mine, and I felt the pressure of him pushing against my palm. I squeezed. His hand was surprisingly warm.

Once we let go, I strode toward one of the front windows facing the street. I flipped up the old window shade, letting in the late morning sunlight. Boy put his paws on my legs, and I picked him up and held him. William stood next to me, the sunlight streaming through him and hitting the floor, where Ghost Cat had returned. She rubbed her head on my leg and purred.

I looked out the window at Salem, Massachusetts.

I had come here looking for an escape.

And I found a family.

Finally, I was home.

Want more Clara and William? Get *Ghost Writer*, Book 2 in the Salem Spirits Cozy Mysteries series, and read how their story continues!

Sign up for Dina Marie's email newsletter and get a Salem Spirits Cozy Mysteries short story for free! Yes, free! Visit dinamariebooks.com for details.

About the Author

Dina Marie is the pen name of award-winning novelist Dina Santorelli, who has been obsessed with all things ghost since . . . well, forever. Married on Halloween, she likes vacationing in spooky cities and visiting cemeteries and haunted hotels. A recent visit to Salem, Massachusetts, in-spired her Salem Spirits series, which she wrote, in part, for her mom, a lover of cozy mystery TV.

www.ingramcontent.com/pod-product-compliance
Lightning Source LLC
Chambersburg PA
CBHW020758310726
48969CB00002B/604